DEAD IN THE DARK

A MADDIE SWALLOWS MYSTERY
BOOK 6

KAT BELLEMORE

KB PRESS

CHOOSE YOUR OWN ADVENTURE: MYSTERY OR ROMANCE

MADDIE SWALLOWS MYSTERIES

Dead Before Dinner

Dead Upon Arrival

Dead Before I Do

Dead Among Stars

Dead by Design

Dead in the Dark

Dead Without a Hitch

BORROWING AMOR: New Mexican Romance

Borrowing Amor

Borrowing Love

Borrowing a Fiancé

Borrowing a Billionaire

Borrowing Kisses

Borrowing Second Chances

STARLIGHT RIDGE: Beach Romance

Diving into Love

Resisting Love

Starlight Love

1
_____

I stood in front of the door, preparing myself for the grisly scene I knew waited just behind it. It was a testament to how bad things had gotten and, without my family's intervention, I wondered how much worse it would have been.

That was the scary thing.

I hadn't even realized what was happening until it was too late.

Anxiety.

It has a habit of sneaking in and making a home without you knowing it. It makes you feel productive, like you can take on the world—while you simultaneously avoid the very thing you should be confronting.

You'd think as a psychologist, I'd be immune to its effects. That I'd be able to see it a mile away.

Unfortunately, I wasn't. Funny thing was, I had noticed

the anxiety. But I'd thought I'd handled it—taken care of it. Said good riddance.

It had only been lurking in the shadows long enough for me to look away, and then it had struck.

I pulled in a long breath, then opened the fridge door.

Four gallon-sized storage bags full of waffles.

Two storage bags of chocolate chip pancakes.

Two containers of spaghetti and meatballs.

A large pizza that had been Frankensteined using leftovers from a pepperoni and green chile, a cheese, a Hawaiian, and a supreme pizza.

One hollowed-out watermelon that contained an inordinate amount of decorative fruit.

I hoped that was all of it.

My fiancé, Benji, came up from behind me and wrapped his arms around my waist. "I just finished putting your and the kids' suitcases in the car. Do you need help in here?"

I turned my head and gave him a quick kiss on the cheek. "I think I can handle it, but I feel so bad. I can't believe all this food is only from the past few days. What a waste."

"And that's just what we couldn't give away," my mom said, walking into the kitchen, her purse slung over one shoulder. I really shouldn't have given her a key. It was meant to be used in times of emergency, but it turned out that my mom had a loose definition of the word.

"What are you doing here?" I asked, pulling out the

pancakes and throwing them into the trashcan I'd set beside me. "We're leaving in a few minutes."

Benji pulled back and gave me a kiss on the forehead before grabbing the bag that held our snacks.

"Just here to make sure you actually take this road trip of yours," she said, wrinkling her nose as I pulled out two-week-old bacon that had been hiding in the back of the fridge.

My kids thundered down the stairs. They weren't so much kids anymore, both out of high school and embarking on new adventures, but they'd always be my little ones, no matter how big they got.

"Of course we're going," my son, Flash, said. "I don't remember the last family vacation we took."

Lilly, the elder child, glanced up from her phone. "I do. It was when we went to the hot air balloon festival a few years ago. Think we'll be able to help the police solve a murder this time too?"

I winced at the thought.

"Absolutely not. We're going to relax and spend *quality* time as a family," I said, pulling out the hollowed-out watermelon. The fruit inside had gone mushy. Into the trash it went. "Got to do it while we can before you two move out. Who knows the next time we'll all be together."

My mom raised a skeptical eyebrow. "That better be all you do while you're gone."

I pulled out several more bags of food and shut the

fridge door. "Why are you so worried? You're the one who suggested this trip in the first place."

She held up her hands in a defensive gesture. "I'm just saying, if you happen upon a dead body, turn around and let someone else deal with it. Like normal people. Otherwise, you'll end up like that Aster Clements guy I keep hearing about on the news."

This coming from the woman who would be first to interrogate everyone in the vicinity.

"Who's Aster Clements?"

My mom got a gleam in her eye. She loved knowing news I didn't. "Get this. The guy is arrested for grand larceny. He says he was questioning his employees about some missing jewelry—about five hundred thousand dollars' worth—when someone anonymously calls the feds and says it was actually Aster himself who stole the jewelry. And they have all the evidence to back it up. Aster claims he's being set up by the guilty employee, but because of an alleged connection to the Flora crime family, he's looking at fifteen years in prison. He says it's all lies, but when you have five hundred thousand dollars' worth of jewelry missing, you go to the FBI, you don't pull the guy into your office and try to talk it out. Only a person who has something to hide does that."

I leaned against the counter, both intrigued and confused. "I'm going to have to follow this story and see how it plays out, but I don't know what any of that has to do with me."

My mom looked at me like it should have been obvious. "Aster tried taking care of things himself. Thought he could handle it on his own. And now look at him. He's no better off than Hagrid—set up for a crime he didn't commit and hauled away to Azkaban."

I gave her a pacifying smile, wondering when she'd finally broken down and read Harry Potter. My kids had been trying to get her to read those books for years. "I'll make sure I'm careful," I promised, then turned my attention to the food spread out on the counter in front of me.

"It's not that I don't trust you to handle yourself in that kind of situation," she said, giving me an equally pacifying smile, though hers was more akin to pity. "But you haven't been yourself lately. Of course, your...issues...have had their perks. For one, I've never seen your bathroom more clean."

"And two?" I asked, immediately regretting it.

She waved a hand at the spaghetti I was shoving down the disposal so it wouldn't go bad while we were gone. "That."

I couldn't deny that I'd gone a bit stir crazy over the past little while, doing everything in my power to keep myself busy and my mind occupied so I didn't have to think about my upcoming nuptials. My fridge was evidence of that.

At first, I'd thrown myself into wedding preparations, and that had worked...for a while. But I'd finished with everything so quickly that I had been left with nothing but to drive myself and everyone else crazy. The result was me cooking more than even my teenage son could eat and organizing every cupboard and closet in the house, even when it wasn't needed.

I liked to think my anxiety was less about getting married for the second time and more that I couldn't wait to spend the rest of my life with my childhood best friend who I'd fallen madly in love with since moving back to my New Mexican hometown.

Now, I was wondering if it was a bit of both.

"Only relaxation allowed," I assured my mom while picking up the pizza box. I hesitated. "Maybe I should leave some food for Trish." I hated to throw away a perfectly good pizza.

Trish had been a godsend when I'd divorced Cameron and moved my family down to the small town of Amor. Trish and I had both been psychology professors at a large university and made the brave, and risky, decision to open our own therapy practice. Trish and her cat, Ava, had moved in with me and the kids, and we'd been one happy family ever since.

Until Benji and I had started dating.

Then, things had begun to feel a bit strained. I'd tried to include Trish in our family activities, but more often than not, she'd excuse herself and say she needed to get to bed early or some nonsense like that.

I'd known Trish a long time, and early bedtimes was

not something she and her bright blue hair were known for.

"She doesn't want your leftover pizza," Flash said, taking the box from me. But instead of throwing it away, he carried it off.

Benji glanced at his phone. "We should probably get going."

I looked into the mostly empty fridge, embarrassed that it had taken my mom forcing me to take a vacation with my family to realize how badly I'd needed this.

"Yes, we should," I said. "Carlsbad Caverns, here we come."

"I'm most interested in the bats," Lilly said, leading us out of the kitchen. "I'm bringing my good camera to see if I can catch them going out to hunt."

"We would never forget about the bats," Benji said, smiling.

He was so good with my kids—I'd never been able to get away with half the stuff he did. When they wouldn't listen to me, he was my reinforcement. And the fact that they were just as excited for us to marry as I was—it made my anxiety melt away and my entire body relax.

Before I could follow my family out the front door, my mom stopped me. "He's a good one," she said.

"I know."

"Of course, he'll never replace me," she continued. "But he's a close second."

There had been times over the past few months when my mom would say little things like that, as if she was afraid that once I was married, I wouldn't need her anymore.

"There's no one like you, Mom," I said truthfully. And for that I was grateful. Since moving back home, I'd come to rely on her more than she'd ever know. Or maybe she did know, and that was why she was worried. Because I would have Benji now.

I nodded toward the front door. "Come on. I'll lock up behind you."

My mom relented and walked ahead of me, but just as I took a step, a blur of gray and white flashed in front of me, and my foot landed right on the tail end of it.

Literally.

Ava leaped into the air, yowling, and her claws came out.

"I'm sorry, but that one's on you," I protested, jumping back.

That cat and I had had a love-hate relationship since the moment Trish and Ava had moved in, and describing it as such was generous. Every chance she got, that cat would sneak-attack me from behind a corner, whack me with her paw, or run off with my keys. Trish swore it wasn't on purpose and that Ava was actually very loving, but that cat had been letting me know for the past few years who was boss, and she wasn't about to stop now.

Ava glared at me, turned her back, and flopped down

in the middle of the entryway, stretching out as far as she could go.

Maybe Trish was right and it wasn't personal, but right then it sure felt like the cat was giving me the middle finger, forcing me to gingerly step around her to get out the door.

I didn't know what Ava was getting so worked up about. As soon as I left, she could stretch out all she wanted. I would be gone for most of the week, spending time with Benji and the kids—the people I loved most.

And nothing was going to ruin it for me.

Not even a cat with a vendetta.

2

"I'm going to throw up."

Those are not the words a mother wants to hear as she's driving switchbacks up a mountain. Especially when before leaving their hotel that mother had cautioned her children the road would likely be full of twists and turns, and she had advised they take medicine. But had those children listened?

One of them had.

The other was suffering because of his inaction, and making the rest of the car worry they'd soon be suffering along with him.

"Flash, you know how easily you get sick," I said, trying to hide my exasperation. *Relaxation*, I told myself. *We are relaxing. Family. Nature. Love.*

Saying calming words did nothing to help when Flash yelled that he needed a bag. Or when his sister was screaming about how gross Flash was and that he shouldn't have eaten all that old pizza.

One hour and a disgusting bag later, we finally arrived at the visitor's center of Carlsbad Caverns.

And I was the opposite of relaxed.

"I'm going to need to have the car professionally cleaned," I told Benji, pacing behind the car. "And I'll probably need to have Flash professionally cleaned while I'm at it. I didn't realize the human stomach could hold that much. But I suppose it explains how he's been able to eat as much as he has over the years."

Benji laughed and pulled me in for a hug. "He's in the bathroom cleaning himself up right now, because you've raised a self-sufficient human who can take care of himself. It's not all on you like when they were younger."

Those had been tough years.

My ex-husband had been more concerned about the goings on at work than at home, which had made things difficult. If only I'd stayed in Amor, I'd have married Benji twenty years earlier.

Of course, Flash and Lilly wouldn't be who they were today without my ex, so I supposed I should be thanking rather than blaming him, though I was okay with doing a little of both.

"You're right," I said, kissing Benji and pulling back. "You always are."

I plastered on a smile, determined to not let a little—or a lot—of throw-up derail my relaxed family vacation.

Once Flash was back and looking his usual self, running around like a rabbit hopped up on sugar, we made our way into the visitor's center.

"Hello," an elderly man said, walking up to us with a smile I couldn't help but return. He was wearing a brown uniform with the logo for the caverns on it and a nametag that said Ralph. "Welcome to Carlsbad Caverns. Is this your first time here?" His eyes were kind, and he seemed genuinely happy to see us.

"Yes, it is," I said. "Any recommendations where to start?"

Ralph nodded toward a desk behind him. "The tours fill up fast, so I'd jump on that. How long are you here for?"

"Three days. Do you think that will be enough time?" I asked, though it didn't matter if it was or not; that was how long we could stay before both Benji and I needed to get back for work.

"Depends on what you mean," Ralph said. "I could sit in those caverns for days and never get tired of them. It's why I choose to volunteer here instead of lying out on a beach somewhere, as if that was what retirement was for." A shout from the other side of the visitor's center gave him pause. "Of course, not everyone loves these caverns like I do."

I turned to see two redheaded women arguing; it looked like maybe they were sisters. "I told you, I'm afraid of the dark," the shorter one said. "I'm not going." Her frizzy hair stuck out from her head as she folded her arms across her chest.

The taller sister threw her hands in the air. "We drove fifteen hours to be here, and it was you who insisted I come with." She paused, her voice softening. "You won't be alone."

Other than the physical resemblance, the two sisters couldn't have been more different. Unlike her shorter sister, everything about this one screamed high fashion. I was certain her outfit cost more than my entire wardrobe. That, combined with her silky hair and slender figure, suggested she had likely done some modeling. Or could, if she so chose.

Ralph held up a finger. "Would you excuse me for a moment?" He scurried over to the two women and was all smiles as he addressed the anxious redhead.

"You know, our self-guided tour is lit the entire way down," he told her in a kind voice. "Perhaps our video in the auditorium can help quell your fears."

The shorter woman's voice shook as she sat down on a bench that looked like it had been created from the cavern rock. "We've already done both, but thank you for the suggestion. Unfortunately, my sister signed us up for one of your guided tours, not realizing it is a wild cave and that turning off the lights is part of the experience. Being that far underground... It won't go well."

Her sister slid onto the bench next to her. "And I told you, I'll be there with you every step of the way, holding your hand. Besides, the darkness only lasts for a moment, right?" She looked to the volunteer for confirmation.

Ralph hesitated, maybe wondering what their definition of a moment was. Ultimately, he settled for, "It's only for a fraction of the time you are down there, and I assure you that you'll be perfectly safe. The bats will be sleeping and your guide won't leave your side for even a second."

The anxious woman whimpered. She turned to her sister. "You want me to go knowing that bats live down there?"

Ralph immediately recognized his mistake. "Only in the deepest of caverns, I assure you."

"Bats," Flash whispered excitedly to Lilly. He turned to me. "Mom, we have to get on that tour."

I looked to Benji, and he looked just as excited as my kids. "Please?" he asked, bringing his hands together as if he were praying.

I laughed. "All right. I'll see if they have any openings, though you'll likely need to wait until tonight to see any bats."

As I waited in line at the desk and overheard several guests being told that today's tour was full, I realized I probably should have preregistered for a tour. Of course, I hadn't known they existed until three minutes earlier.

When it was finally my turn, a steely eyed man in an olive-green uniform greeted me with a quick hello, then fell silent, apparently waiting for me to tell him what I needed. It was a stark contrast to the kind volunteer.

"I realize this is short notice," I started, "but I wondered if my family could do a guided tour sometime in the next three days."

The man's lips dipped into a frown. "Impossible. Our tours have been sold out for months. The best you can do is purchase your park passes and go on the self-guided tour."

I hesitated and glanced back at my family. They were looking around at a variety of exhibits, their expressions open and full of wonder. I turned back to the man. "You don't want to check to see if there have been any last-minute cancellations?" I thought of the redheads. "Maybe someone who is afraid of the dark?"

The man didn't so much as glance at his computer. "Our tours are full."

Okey-dokey. "I guess I'll need four park passes, then," I said, disappointed, and I rummaged in my purse for my wallet. You'd think that national park employees would be required to have at least somewhat of an approachable personality, if not friendly.

As I walked away, passes in hand, a young woman took the man's place behind the counter. "Thanks, Eric. I know you have a tour to lead, but I couldn't hold it anymore. Whoever said I should drink eight cups of water a day must have unlimited bathroom breaks."

So, the man didn't usually sell tickets—he was a ranger. I felt bad for his next tour.

Eric gave the woman a small nod and a hint of a smile,

and then left to attend to whatever duties he had elsewhere. Seemed he had a heart after all, or at the very least a Grinch-sized one. Maybe his too could grow three sizes, as in Dr. Seuss's beloved children's book. Though I doubted it would be in time to get us tickets.

Flash bounded over to me. "So, when does our tour start?"

I hated to give my family the bad news. There had to be other ways to procure tickets for the guided tours. Who knew, maybe there was something Ralph could do to help us out. By the time I'd turned to where the volunteer had been standing moments earlier, though, both he and the redheads had disappeared.

That had been my plan B, and I didn't have a plan C. Before I could confess that I hadn't planned ahead and had been unsuccessful in securing us a spot on a tour, a man to my right spoke in my stead. He was short and sported a goatee that he likely thought looked good, but it really just made him look like he'd forgotten to shave. Judging by his olive-green shirt and nametag, he was another park ranger.

"You're here for the guided tour of the King's Palace?"

"We sure are," Flash said, excitedly bouncing on his toes.

The man smiled. "Take the elevator from the gift shop and down to the underground rest area."

Oh, dear. My family was already making their way to the gift shop, and it left me unsure what to do. Family vacations weren't something we did often, and I had no idea when the next opportunity would present itself. I didn't want to let them down.

I turned to the cheerful woman who now stood behind the ticket counter.

"I'm sorry," I said. "I know I should have planned ahead, but my family has really been looking forward to going on a guided tour while we're here. Do you have four available spaces sometime in the next three days?"

Unlike Ranger Eric, the woman gave me a kind smile. "Let me see what I can do." As her fingers flew over her keyboard, she glanced at me. "Our King's Palace tour has been the only tour open for several years because of flooding, so it's been highly sought after. And for good reason. Our rangers can take you places you can't go on your own. It's pretty spectacular, as long as you don't think about how deep you are under the earth's surface."

Uh-huh. "And how deep does that King's Palace tour go?" I asked, suddenly hesitant. I was tempted to tell her she didn't need to look for additional tour openings and that we'd be fine exploring on our own.

"Eight hundred thirty feet below the desert surface," she said, squinting at her screen. "The path gets pretty steep in some places."

Eight hundred. That was...a lot.

"However, we just opened up our Lower Cave tour again, and not many people are aware of it. I might be able to find you something there. We only go down there three times a week, though, so no promises."

"That's all right. I appreciate your help."

She straightened, sporting a wide smile. "You're in luck. I have space tomorrow morning. You could do the self-guided tour through the Big Room today, and then show up back here at eight-thirty tomorrow morning for the Lower Cave. It is a three-hour tour, so you will want to be on time for orientation. You'll also need to dress warm and wear shoes that have good traction. Something that will support the ankle, you know?"

Three hours. That was a lot of time to spend under-ground. *It's for the family*, I reminded myself, and handed over my credit card as she printed off our tickets.

"For the self-guided tour, you can either go back outside to the main cave entrance and hike down, or go straight through the gift shop and down the elevator," she said, then gave me a small wave. "Enjoy!"

By the looks of it, Benji and the kids had already gone down, so I'd need to take the elevator this time. Probably better that way, considering we'd be hiking for several hours the next day.

Of course, I hadn't realized what taking the elevator had meant.

There was no bright, cheerful elevator music. Instead, metal enclosed me as I stepped inside. The sterile-looking doors closed slowly, and the car lurched as it began its descent, narrow windows in the walls giving me a view of the rock as it whizzed by. Pure limestone, according to a brochure I'd picked up in the gift shop.

And the elevator didn't stop. With each second, my stomach inched toward my throat and I had to close my eyes. I was beginning to wonder if it would ever end when, a full minute later, the elevator slowed, and with a cheerful ding, the doors opened. And I was still alive. Mostly.

As I stepped out, however, I realized the elevator was just the beginning.

3

"Mom," Flash yelled across the open expanse that stretched before me. My gaze landed on him, wildly waving his arms to get my attention. He, Lilly, and Benji stood next to a souvenir stand, of all things.

I couldn't believe it. We were surrounded on all sides by rock, and yet in this open cavern, there was a place you could buy snacks. There were also tables and chairs to eat them at, and bathrooms. I supposed if you hiked all the way down, you'd already have been walking close to an hour and would need some sort of reprieve.

Flash yelled out to me again, and I walked over.

"The ranger needs our tickets," he said. "And you have to promise to take a shower and wash our clothes after. Something about a disease going around and not wanting to get the bats sick."

"That's right," the ranger said, turning to me. "It's

called…" I hadn't noticed him—the man at the counter from earlier, Eric—standing a few feet away, speaking with an elderly couple. His words faltered, and his lips dipped into a frown. "Look, I'm sorry, I know you want to be on this tour. But you really should have planned your trip better. It's full."

I waved the tickets in the air. "I know. These are for tomorrow."

His eyebrows rose, and he took the tickets from me, studying them, as if I were trying to pull a fast one on him.

"Looks like you got lucky," he finally said. He didn't seem pleased about it, and I wondered why it mattered to him who went on a tour or how we'd managed to procure tickets.

Eric held a hand to his mouth and loudly said, "Two minutes until the King's Palace tour begins. If you are on this tour, please use the bathroom and have a water bottle handy because there are no drinking fountains where we're going."

A wave of chuckles circulated around us.

"We're not on this one," I told Benji. "Best I could do was a tour first thing tomorrow morning. But we can explore the Big Room while we're down here. Whatever that is." I handed him my purse. "First things first, though. Bathroom." That girl behind the desk was right. Drinking too much water definitely had its pitfalls.

When I entered the bathroom, I nearly ran over two women who were standing in the entryway near the sinks.

The redheads. Looked like Ralph, the elderly volunteer, had been able to work his magic after all.

"I don't want to be here," the anxious one was saying, her lips trembling. "Let's just go."

Her sister, on the other hand, looked more determined than ever. "Jasmine, you know how important this is. If you return home and you didn't even try..." She paused and closed her eyes, like she didn't want to think about what that would mean. After a beat, she opened them again. "He can't avoid you here—not when he's trapped on a tour a thousand feet underground."

"It will turn ugly," Jasmine whispered, her eyes wide and scared. "I don't know if I can do it."

"He's dangerous," her sister said, her eyes narrowing. "Think of the consequences."

Jasmine nodded slowly. "You're right."

When they turned to leave, their expressions opened in surprise, like they had thought they'd been alone, then stepped around me with tight smiles. It left me wondering what kind of drama that King's Palace tour was in for today. I kind of wished we were on it.

THE BIG ROOM. The national park hadn't exactly been creative when naming this cavern. It turned out that this particular "room" was the length of six football fields and was the largest single chamber in the U.S. It felt like it too, by the time we were done exploring it. That wasn't to say it wasn't incredible and amazing and I didn't love every minute of it. I even managed to forget how deep we were underground for the next couple of hours as Lilly took an excessive number of pictures of the various formations.

But my legs were exhausted by the time we were finished, and I wondered how I was ever going to make it through a three-hour tour the following morning. What we needed was an early night's sleep. We could watch the bats another day.

I woke up early the next morning, my mind racing as I imagined what might await us on our guided tour. Whatever we encountered, I wanted to ensure I was prepared. My legs had recovered from their escapade through the Big Room (mostly), I had my hiking shoes that said *I mean business*, and I was equipped with a brand-new hydration backpack that meant I could drink water out of a convenient tube for the duration of the tour. I obviously hadn't thought about the bathroom situation at the time, or I might have reconsidered the purchase.

As it turned out, even with my shoes and hydration pack, I wasn't close to being prepared for the adventure we were about to embark on, and, had I known what I'd signed my family up for, I would have canceled.

But I didn't, so we showed up at exactly 8:30 a.m., refreshed and anxious to get going. I'd used the bathroom and then ensured the rest of my family all had water bottles, good shoes, and jackets. Well, everyone had a jacket except Flash. Was it only my boy who insisted on wearing shorts and T-shirts throughout the winter?

The same woman from the previous day was behind the counter, and she lit up when we walked into the visitor's center. "Welcome back," she said. "Orientation is down this hall, first door on your right. Have fun down there!"

The way she said it, with a smile that was a little too wide—like she was in on a secret we weren't—it made me nervous.

"Thanks," Lilly said, picking up the pace and leading us down the hallway to the orientation room.

I had expected a typical classroom with chairs and long tables. There were certainly those, but there were also several shelves holding miner's helmets with headlamps attached. I wondered if that was typical for guided tours. I hadn't noticed anyone else wearing them in the caverns the previous day.

And then the one ranger I'd rather not be our guide walked in. Eric. Maybe he'd be in a better mood today.

From all appearances, he was. He smiled as he spoke with a middle-aged man wearing a pullover sweatshirt. Of course, that smile dipped when we walked in, but it quickly returned.

Maybe his reaction yesterday had more to do with us

than him having a rough day, but I couldn't imagine why. We hadn't done anything but ask to go on a guided tour.

"Mom, look how cool I look," Flash called to me. He'd made a beeline to the helmets and snapped one on, now walking toward me as if he were on a fashion runway. "Think we get to wear these on our tour?"

Ranger Eric frowned. "Yes, you do. They were all sanitized last night, so I guess that one is yours."

"Awesome!"

Flash had always struggled with social cues, as well as impulsivity. Now that he was going to be striking out on his own, I was left with the impression that I hadn't done enough to help him in those areas. I supposed I'd thought he'd grow out of it.

"Thank you," I said, and it caught Eric off guard. He grunted, then turned back to the man he'd been speaking with, his smile returning.

Next to enter the orientation room was a young couple. No wedding rings. They seemed a mismatch from the start, him with tattoos covering his arms and his dark hair cropped short, while his companion wore a color-coordinated exercise outfit in bright pinks and greens. And even though her hair was pulled up into a ponytail, it was in a way that made it look like she'd spent far longer on it than she should have.

When the young man tried to take the woman's hand, she artfully avoided it by reaching for her water bottle. Interesting.

Ranger Eric turned to address the room. "We're waiting on three others, and then we can begin." Just as he finished speaking, his gaze landed on the doorway, and in walked the two redheads from yesterday. It hadn't been the King's Palace tour they'd been talking about—it had been this one.

So. I hadn't missed any of the drama yesterday. I shouldn't have been as excited as I was at this revelation—I prided myself on not being a gossip like everyone else in my small town.

Regardless, this tour had just gotten more interesting.

The nervous one from yesterday, Jasmine, didn't look like her anxiety had decreased at all. Her gaze jumped around the room, landing first on Ranger Eric, then the young couple, us, then back to Eric.

If anyone in the group recognized her, they didn't say anything. Ranger Eric motioned for everyone to have a seat just as another ranger entered the room. He appeared to be the polar opposite of Eric—young, skinny, and all smiles.

"Welcome to orientation for the Lower Cave tour," Ranger Eric said. "This is my colleague, Ranger Charlie. He's new to Carlsbad Caverns, and this will be his second time in the Lower Cave. He is training for future tours like this one. As you might know, this tour has been closed for quite some time due to flooding, and you are some of the first guests to return. What an awesome experience you are about to have."

The young tattooed man raised his hand. "Why is there an orientation for this tour but not the King's Palace?"

Ranger Eric hesitated, his gaze scanning the group. "Do any of you know what the Lower Cave is?"

All of us looked at each other, then shook our heads.

Eric released a long sigh and rubbed his eyebrows, like this was going to be the longest tour of his life. "Okay, let's do some quick introductions to help you all feel comfortable with each other, and then we'll talk about expectations."

He gestured to the young couple. "Why don't we start here? Names and where you're from will suffice."

The tattooed man, probably in his mid-twenties, was watching the guy with the pullover sweatshirt with a curious expression, almost like he recognized him but couldn't for the life of him remember where they'd met.

"I'm Thomas, and I'm studying geology at the University of Utah," he said slowly, though as he spoke, his expression brightened. "As much as I love the diversity of landscape we have up north, we don't have anything like this. Seriously, this place is so cool. We've already hiked down from the main entrance and then through the Big Room. The stalactites and the—"

His female companion placed a hand on his arm with a small laugh. "They already know, honey. They're here experiencing the same thing you are." She quickly removed her hand as she turned to us. "I'm Amber, and even though I go to school in Utah, I'm from California."

Eric nodded. "Welcome." He gestured to the redheads.

Jasmine didn't answer right away, her gaze settling on Thomas. He seemed completely oblivious to it, his attention absorbed by the equipment surrounding us.

Her sister, seeming annoyed, forced a smile. "I'm Violet, and this is my sister, Jasmine. Yes, our parents have an unhealthy fascination with flowers, and no, we aren't twins. She's older by a year, and we are originally from South Dakota."

"You're a long way from home," Eric said. He seemed to be looking at a spot just past the sisters rather than directly at them, and I wondered if they somehow made him nervous. "Welcome."

Mr. Harding was next. His chestnut brown hair was slicked back, a contrast to the shorts he wore with his pullover sweatshirt. He adjusted his glasses as he introduced himself as a journalist from Albuquerque, but we were to ignore that fact and treat him as if he were any other New Mexican who didn't know how to dress appropriately for the weather. Flash laughed at that and held up his hand, likely because he himself was wearing shorts and a T-shirt, despite my insistence he at least bring a sweatshirt. Mr. Harding complied and high fived him.

His being a journalist explained why Ranger Eric was suddenly all smiles any time he spoke—had to give a good impression of the national park, after all.

And then there was us.

"I'm Maddie," I began. "We're from New Mexico as

well. These are my children, Flash and Lilly. Flash graduated high school early, so we wanted to get in a last family
vacation before they both move away."

"My mom and Benji are getting married," Flash
announced, continuing my introduction. He pointed to
Benji. "That's Benji. He's a handyman, and he can fix
anything. My grandma told us to come on this trip because
my mom's freaking out about the wedding and made like a
truckload of waffles and spaghetti last week. We're hoping
this calms her down, and—"

I clamped my hand over his mouth and pulled him
into a tight hug. "And we're so excited to be here." I gave
everyone a strained smile and didn't let go of Flash until he
stopped squirming.

This was an indication that either he'd given up the
fight or he'd lost consciousness. Thankfully it was the
former. When I finally released him and leaned back in
my chair, he gave me an accusatory glare.

"What did you do that for? It's all true."

"That doesn't mean everyone else has to know," I said
in a fierce whisper.

Ranger Eric, for once, looked at us without his usual
annoyance. Instead, he seemed quite amused. I supposed
that was better than the alternative, even if it was at our
expense.

"Thank you," he said, his attention returning to the rest
of the group. "This is a smaller group than we're used to
having on this tour, and it will absolutely be to your advan-

tage." He held up a finger. "Quick question: Have any of you visited other caves during your stay here? Other than the Big Room."

Lilly gave a quick shake of her head. "We just arrived yesterday."

After receiving the same answer from the rest of the group, Ranger Eric gave a satisfied nod. "Great. Then let's talk about bats."

Jasmine whimpered, looking like she was ready to bolt from the room. Her sister held Jasmine in her seat and said to the ranger, "You might want to talk quickly, or you're going to have an even smaller group than you anticipated."

4

Ranger Eric gave Jasmine a wary look, like he wouldn't mind if she escaped and he didn't have to spend the next three hours talking her down from her panic attacks.

His attention turned to the rest of us. "I want to talk a little about our bats and the danger they are in." He paused to study our group, as if to convey how important this conversation was going to be. "White-nose syndrome. It is a cold-loving fungus that invades bats' skin where it's not covered by fur, and it has been spreading through the United States and killing millions of bats. It isn't dangerous to humans, but it attacks the bats during hibernation and may be causing them to starve or become dehydrated. We haven't observed white-nose syndrome here at Carlsbad Caverns, but because of its seriousness, in an attempt to stop its spread, I ask that as you leave the cave today, you walk the length of the bio-cleaning mat to remove any spores you may have picked up along the way. If you plan on visiting any other caves while here at Carlsbad Caverns, you will need to change your clothes in between visits and decontaminate your footwear with supplies I will provide you with at the end of the tour." He pulled in a long breath, like that had taken a lot out of him. "Any questions?"

His gaze landed on the reporter. "Mr. Harding?"

Mr. Harding adjusted his glasses and patted down his hair, though with the amount of gel he'd used, it wasn't going anywhere. "Not at the moment. Conduct your tour as usual. I'll save any unanswered questions for the end."

Ranger Eric's gaze lingered for another long second, then moved to the rest of us. "Anyone else?"

Our group was silent, all excitement for the tour subdued by the prospect of us inadvertently spreading disease and killing entire populations of bats.

"Okay, then let's talk expectations. Only a fraction of the thousands of people who visit Carlsbad Caverns will have the opportunity to visit the Lower Cave, and that is very much on purpose. This is a wild cave. That means there is no permanent lighting down there, hence the helmets." He gestured toward the large rack holding at least a dozen of them. "There is not a paved path like you'll find when exploring the Big Room, and in order to get into the cave, you will need to do a short rappel and descend three metal ladders. There are pools of water throughout the cave, and some of the rock can be a bit slick. There are also narrow passages you'll need to work your way through. This isn't just a tour. It's an adventure."

While my heart quickened in anticipation, Jasmine's complexion paled. I worried for her and wondered why she was on this tour in the first place. Coming to the caves at all seemed to cause her distress, but this? This was just torture.

"Let's quickly form a line, and I'll check your footwear before you grab a helmet," Ranger Eric said, stepping back and allowing room for us to gather up front.

I got up from my seat at the table, but rather than jump into the growing line, I slid in next to Jasmine and her sister farther down the table. They didn't look like they'd be joining the rest of the group anytime soon.

"Hi, Jasmine. I'm Maddie."

Jasmine gave me a wary look and nodded. "The mom from New Mexico."

I gave her a smile. "Yes, but I'm also a psychologist, and I couldn't help but notice that you seem a bit anxious about the tour. How are you holding up?"

Violet snorted. "A bit anxious? I hope they can fit a stretcher down there, because she's going to pass out within the first ten minutes."

Jasmine shot Violet a glare but didn't say anything.

"No one would think less of you if you chose not to go down there," I told Jasmine, attempting the calmest voice I could without being patronizing. "It's a wild cave, after all, and just coming to the caves at all was a brave thing to do. Your value as a human being doesn't hinge on whether you rappel underground or merely walk through the park and enjoy the magnificent views from the surface."

Lilly had joined the line to get her helmet but was looking at me and swiping her hand in a cutting motion across her throat, trying to tell me to cut it out and leave Jasmine alone. It embarrassed my kids when I attempted impromptu therapy sessions in public places, and they always gave me the look she was right now—the one that said she wanted me to stop. Immediately. That random people didn't like strangers intruding on their business.

But then tears sprang to Jasmine's eyes. "You're right," she said. "I'm actually a really brave person. I singlehandedly started my own business, which is thriving, and more recently, I had the guts to end a relationship with a man I thought would be my forever person."

Violet opened her mouth, as if to stop Jasmine from saying anything further, like she shouldn't be sharing these personal details with a random woman.

There had been no need, though, because Jasmine straightened, her eyes hardening. "And that's why I need to finish what I started."

She stood up, and her eyes softened as she turned her gaze on me. "Thank you, Maddie. You're very good at what you do."

I sometimes felt like a fraud—like I really only provided a listening ear and an opportunity for my clients to discover what they already knew. But if that was what they needed, I was happy to help.

I returned her smile and stood. "Anytime. I have worked with people with some pretty intense fears. If you find yourself in trouble down there, you just let me know."

"Of course. And thank you again." Jasmine then joined the line.

"I really wish you wouldn't have done that. She might actually go through with it now," Violet muttered, before chasing after her sister, leaving me looking on with confusion.

THE SMALL GATE we stood in front of might have looked innocent to most. To me? It could have been a gateway to Hell, for all I knew. The only thing that lay beyond it was slick rock that plunged into darkness. And we were expected to walk through it. Ranger Eric had taken the lead, with Ranger Charlie bringing up the rear, and we were instructed to turn on our headlamps. They didn't help.

The gate opened with a creak, and I swallowed back my own fear. Benji must have sensed my anxiety, because he slipped his hand in mine. "Different type of adventure than you're used to, eh?"

"A bit." I squeezed his hand in an attempt to settle my heart.

Ranger Eric turned to the group. "Who would like to go first?"

Thomas volunteered, an eager look on his face. He inched forward, then turned so he faced us. Taking hold of a long knotted rope, he walked backwards, his feet spread out and his headlamp illuminating the steep decline. When he reached the bottom, I realized it wasn't as difficult or as far as I'd expected, and I volunteered to go next, wanting to get it over with. Thomas's girlfriend, Amber, seemed grateful, as she now looked like she was having her own doubts.

The rope was scratchy in my hands as I spread my feet out and slowly walked backwards down the rock. I hated the feeling of not being able to see where I was going and was quite slow as I kept looking over my shoulder to make sure nothing hazardous was behind me. Of course, it continued to be nothing but rock and darkness until I got to a point where I no longer needed the rope and could join Thomas at the bottom.

"Quite the hike, huh?" Thomas said. "A guy at work told me I should bring my girlfriend here as a joke, only I thought he was serious. I guess he thought I couldn't handle this type of thing. You can bet I'll be taking a lot of pictures while I'm down here to prove him wrong. In fact, will you take one of me now?"

I smiled, already liking the guy. He was the type of person I'd love Flash to befriend once he was out in the real world, when I could no longer protect him. As long as they didn't convince Flash to get matching tattoos. Those seemed kind of permanent. "Of course."

By the time we finished with our photo session, the rest of the hikers had made their way down. Flash and Lilly pushed their way to the front of the pack, eagerly looking ahead to what might be next.

What was next was crawling through tight spaces so we could access ladders that would take us farther down into the cave. Three metal ladders, to be exact. It was at the first ladder that Jasmine nearly turned back. To her credit, it was pretty sketchy, and I found myself having doubts as well. Thankfully, the following ladders were much easier.

And then we were there. Sort of. Honestly, it was difficult to know where "here" was. There was no giant room like we'd walked through the previous day. Instead, we found ourselves in a maze and, without permanent lighting, it felt raw—like we were the first ones to discover it. Or it would have except for the red tape that had been placed on the ground to create a makeshift path.

"Here's where you put your gloves on," Ranger Eric instructed from the front.

The latex gloves weren't to keep our hands warm—though I certainly wished they would—they were to make sure the oils from our skin didn't damage the formations that surrounded us. It would be a tragedy of the highest form, because this place was incredible. It truly felt wild—like a place that time had forgotten. Stalactites looked like they were pouring from the ceiling, and formations rose from the ground as if by the hand of an ancient god.

The farther we went, the colder the air became, and I wrapped my arms around my waist to try to keep warm. I had worn a thin sweater, not expecting winter-like temperatures. Or at least, winter in New Mexico. Looked like Flash hadn't been the only one unprepared.

Lilly had of course brought her camera and was at the back of the pack, stopping every few feet to take another picture, her only light coming from our headlamps, which were constantly moving.

At some point I looked down and noticed the red tape was no longer guiding our path. I slowed my steps and waited for Lilly to catch up, not wanting to risk her losing her way. Even though Ranger Charlie was behind the pack, this was only his second time being down here, so I doubted he'd be of much help.

"At this rate, we're never going to make it out of this place," I told her with a laugh.

"I can't help it," Lilly said, stopping to take another picture. "This place is incredible. Everywhere I look, there is a new formation that looks completely different from the ones next to it. How is all of this even possible?"

As if Ranger Eric had heard Lilly's question, he motioned for the group to gather in front of him. His lips turned down when he saw how far back Lilly and I were.

"I could stay down here forever," Thomas was saying to

Amber as we caught up. "I mean, have you ever seen anything so beautiful?"

I didn't hear her response, distracted by movement to my right.

Jasmine was moving along the periphery of the room, and she seemed to have no interest in the formations that surrounded her.

"Please stay close," Ranger Eric said. "It would seem the taped path has not been completed as it was supposed to be, and I can't have any of you getting lost on me." He seemed more concerned than annoyed by this, and he momentarily lost his concentration before his attention quickly returned to us. "How is all this possible?" He gestured around the space where we stood, his voice soft. "Have you ever seen anything that compares to the incredible number of stalactites above you?"

Thomas's mouth gaped open as he looked about him. "I never thought I'd be so lucky. Did you know that as the water seeps through the rock, it deposits layer upon layer of calcite?" he said. "It creates formations and stalactites and all the amazing things in these caves. The draperies and the soda straws. They grow incredibly slow, but as long as there is calcium bicarbonate-rich water seeping through the limestone, the formations will continue to grow."

Amber elbowed him in the side. "No one likes a showoff."

Eric chuckled. "Looks like I'll be out of a job soon." He

nodded toward the ceiling. "Currently, only about five percent of the formations are actively growing, considering the desert above. The last time one hundred percent of the formations would have been actively growing was in a period of glaciation. What we see in the rings inside the formations are the coming and going of ice ages."

Flash turned to me, his mouth splitting into a wide grin. "This is so cool. And we haven't even gotten to see the bats yet."

Benji leaned forward, a sparkle in his eyes. "Just don't let them drink your blood."

Lilly smirked. "That's vampire bats. I doubt they have any of those here."

Jasmine had rejoined the group and raised a tentative hand, as if unsure if she was allowed to ask a question. "But how could anyone have discovered these caves? We're so far beneath the surface." Her voice quivered, like just the thought of it was enough to give her a panic attack.

Ranger Eric's smile widened. He looked genuinely excited about the question, and I realized that he really did want to be here. Maybe his people skills left a lot to be desired, but he genuinely cared about these caves.

Mr. Harding stepped up next to me with his phone out, seeming eager to also know the answer. "I have permission," he assured me. "Signed all the appropriate forms." And then he pressed a giant red button to begin recording.

"Can I answer this one?" Ranger Charlie said from the back.

Ranger Eric did a double take, almost like he'd forgotten the ranger-in-training had joined the tour. He didn't look like he wanted to hand over the reins to someone so new, but likely not wanting to appear ungracious, he gestured for Charlie to continue.

Charlie eagerly made his way to the front and then lowered his voice, as if he were telling a ghost story around a campfire. To his credit, that honestly felt like what we were doing down here. Ghost hunting.

"Imagine over a hundred years ago, Jim White, a sixteen-year-old boy, exploring on his own with nothing but the light from a lantern," Charlie said. "Jim could see basic shapes and outlines, but he wouldn't have been able to see the caverns the way we do. Just as sailors use the stars to navigate the ocean, Jim used the formations to navigate these caves, and he gave these formations names to help him find his way out. It wouldn't be until 1917, when a man by the name of Ray Davis came down into the caves with young Jim and took the first flash photography, that Jim would truly understand what he had discovered. And it would be these photographs that would introduce the rest of the world to Carlsbad Caverns."

"All because of photography," Lilly whispered with a solemn nod.

I stifled a smile. When I'd moved to Amor with my kids, I'd never have dreamed that my daughter's habit of recording a daily video diary would blossom into a passion for film and photography. She would be leaving soon for a full-time photography job in California, and she had plans to make documentaries on the side.

I couldn't be prouder.

I pulled her into a side hug, wishing I could make these moments last longer.

"Jim understood the dangers of exploring these caves," Ranger Charlie continued, his voice now barely above a whisper. "He originally named some of the formations things like Devil's Spring, Devil's Den, and Witch's Fingers. And it makes sense. Everything he encountered was shrouded in darkness —the cave's natural state. A fact you can't fully appreciate without experiencing it yourself." He gave a dramatic pause. "Brace yourselves, because things are about to get dark."

Even though Jasmine stood on the opposite side of the group, I heard her whimper. Her sister linked arms with her and gave her a reassuring smile.

"Uh, we don't do the blackout yet. I usually wait for the Rookery," Ranger Eric said.

Even in the limited light, I could see Charlie's cheeks redden. "Oh, sorry. I guess I got carried away. I memorized the manual," he said with a sheepish smile.

Ranger Eric released a sigh. "With such a great setup, we might as well do it now. Want to say your last line again, Charlie? And then as he says 'dark,' we'll all turn off our headlamps, okay?"

That made Ranger Charlie's day, and his smile widened into a grin, as if he couldn't believe his good luck.

It made me like Ranger Eric just a little more than I had. All things considered, the man was growing on me.

"Brace yourselves," Charlie said again. "Because things are about to get dark."

And just like that, we were plunged into darkness.

Except, darkness didn't begin to describe what we were experiencing. It went beyond lack of light. The blackness that had encased us felt thick and heavy. Like someone was sitting on my chest.

Time seemed to slow, and I wondered when we could turn our lights back on. If I was struggling this badly, I couldn't imagine how difficult it must be for Jasmine in this moment.

"Wave your hand in front of your face," Eric said, his disembodied voice floating through the void.

I did as he requested, but it was as if my hand didn't exist. I had never experienced true darkness until this moment. No matter how long we stayed in the dark, no matter how many minutes passed, our eyes didn't adjust. It would be like this forever.

My heart rate increased, and I instinctively sought out Benji's hand. I couldn't find it.

"Can we turn the lights back on now?" Jasmine's voice held panic, like she was going to lose it if someone didn't do something fast.

But Eric didn't respond. Instead, we were met with the sound of a groan, followed by a thud.

"Ranger Eric?" a different voice said. It sounded like Violet.

Silence.

"Mom?" Flash said from somewhere next to me. "I think something's wrong with our guide."

Yes, I'd had a similar thought.

"Shield your eyes," I said, knowing that the sudden brightness from my headlamp would be painful. I clicked it on, and it took some time for my eyes to adjust.

Even then, I couldn't find Ranger Eric.

"He's here." Amber's panicked voice rang through the cave. We all took an involuntary step away from Amber, and that was when I saw him, crumpled in a pile on the floor of the cave.

"He must have slipped and fallen," Thomas said, his voice trembling. He nodded to several standing pools of water nearby. I hadn't noticed water on the cave floor in front of us, but I supposed it was possible it had been slick where the ranger had been standing.

"How are we going to get him the help he needs?" Lilly asked. "That's a long way back, and I don't think we can carry him through some of those tight spaces, let alone up the ladders."

That was an important question, but it wasn't the biggest issue at hand.

How were we going to find our way out of the cave without a guide?

5

The gravity of our situation hit everyone at the same time.

"We're going to die down here," Jasmine said, her voice so high-pitched, it caused me physical pain.

Amber folded her arms, squinting against the light as one by one everyone turned their headlamps back on. "No one is going to die, so please stop with the drama. You'll only make the situation worse."

"It's a natural reaction," Thomas said. "Even I'm beginning to feel a bit nervous."

Amber harrumphed, and Jasmine began crying.

I turned, my gaze searching out Ranger Charlie, who was now in charge of this tour. He stood near us, staring at Eric as if he were in shock.

"Ranger Charlie, what do you need us to do?" I asked.

When Charlie didn't answer right away, Mr. Harding

touched him on the shoulder, sending Charlie a foot in the air as he yelped. He was no longer the young and carefree man he'd been ten minutes earlier. Now his eyes had a wild look about them, his gaze darting from person to person.

"Are you okay?" I asked gently, taking a small step toward him. "I know this must be quite the shock."

Charlie aggressively shook his head. "No. I'm not okay. I'm in charge now. Me. As if I know anything. To make matters worse, Eric was the one with the radio, and look." He pointed to a broken black radio on the ground that must have smashed against the cave floor when Eric had fallen. "And there was supposed to be red tape marking the path so we knew where was safe to walk. It was here a couple of days ago. But do you see red tape anywhere? It wouldn't be so bad if there was another tour coming through in a couple hours. Not with this one. Two days."

We were losing Charlie. His breaths came fast, and I was afraid he'd hyperventilate and we'd have two men to carry out before the day was through.

"Surely someone will realize we're missing before then," I said, taking long breaths and attempting to keep myself from spiraling to where Charlie had already gone.

I noticed another light to my right. It wasn't a headlamp, though. It was the dull light of a screen that had been shoved in someone's pocket.

Mr. Harding was still recording.

"Maybe this part of the tour shouldn't make it into your article," I said in his direction. I nodded to his lit pocket.

"Events that are recorded are no longer susceptible to human interpretation, and then we, as witnesses, have no choice but to yield to what actually occurred, rather than what we merely thought occurred," he said, his voice gruff.

"Our guide has been injured and deserves our respect. I doubt you'd appreciate if every embarrassing moment of your life was recorded for others to listen to, watch, rehash, and poke fun at. You know how social media is nowadays." I shook my head. "Please pretend to not be a journalist for a few minutes and act like an empathetic human being." I then turned my attention back to Ranger Charlie, knowing that Mr. Harding had no intention of listening to me.

I wasn't usually this forward, on the brink of being rude, but I had made plenty of mistakes in my life, and living in a small town meant that everyone made sure I knew it. Nothing went unnoticed. I hoped to save this poor man from a similar fate, even if he hadn't been my favorite person in the world.

Mr. Harding hesitated, then surprised me by pulling his phone out of his pocket and pressing the red square. "You're right. And I'm sorry. I'll do something actually useful and see if I can find a clear path out of here."

Well, that was a pleasant surprise, but it was short-lived before Flash called to me, "Mom, I don't think he fell."

I turned to my son. He and Benji were leaning over

Eric, looking at him from all angles while Lilly took pictures. We were a bona fide family crime scene team.

"What do you have?" I asked, walking over.

Benji pointed to the ground near Eric's feet. "There's no water where Eric was, and his shoes look new with deep treads. He's not going to just slip."

My heart stalled. "You think someone did this."

Flash pointed to the wound on the back of Eric's head. "This was likely where he fell and hit his head."

Benji pointed to a spot on the side closest to him. "So then why is there another wound?"

I leaned forward and saw what Benji was referring to. "Two wounds in different locations from falling and hitting his head," I said. "Not likely."

Benji dropped his voice to a whisper. "Not unless someone helped him. Maddie, I checked for a pulse. I can't find one."

This was no longer a tragic accident. It was murder. Poor Eric.

My gaze scanned the ground as I straightened. And there it was. A flashlight. I moved in to get a closer look but kept my distance, not wanting to touch it and disturb the evidence. There were visible traces of blood on the edge.

Not wanting to cause panic, I walked back and crouched next to Benji. "Found it. A flashlight. Ranger Eric likely brought it along as a backup to his headlamp." I nodded toward an empty loop on the ranger's belt. "Someone here knew Eric before this tour, and apparently, they weren't his biggest fan. What better place to kill him than a thousand feet underground? Too bad they didn't think things through, leaving everyone, including themselves, stranded."

Benji gave me a grim smile. "Maybe they didn't realize the second park ranger would be a trainee."

"I should have brought my fingerprint kit with me," Flash said with a frustrated shake of his head. "I know what our vacations are like."

I was about to deny it but then stopped. It was true. Everywhere I went, dead bodies followed.

"Wouldn't help," I said, turning my attention back to my family. "We're all wearing gloves. No fingerprints."

Lilly lowered her camera. "So, we have a body. A murder weapon. No fingerprints. No security cameras. And no way out. Which means...we're trapped underground with a murderer."

My daughter had tried to keep her voice low, but it wasn't low enough.

"Did you just say we're trapped with a murderer?" Violet asked, her own volume rising a few decibels. She was supposed to be the one keeping her sister calm, but it was going to be difficult to keep anyone from freaking out now.

Amber, who had done her best to keep physical contact with her boyfriend at a minimum, now clutched onto Thomas like her life depended on it. Who knew, maybe it did. "I never should have allowed you to drag me down here. You knew this isn't my type of vacation. Give me sunshine. A beach. But caves and bats? Not my idea of a good time. And now this."

"I told you, a guy at work guaranteed it would be the adventure of a lifetime," Thomas said. "Who wouldn't want that?"

Amber frowned and released Thomas's arm. "Yes, and you believe everything you are told. You believed the random elderly woman who called asking for a donation because she needed a medical procedure done, only to have your bank account drained. You believed the guy at the bar who told you if you drink eleven beers, it's considered good luck and you'd ace your gemology exam the next day, only you passed out after four drinks and missed the exam entirely. I wouldn't be surprised if you're on a list of the world's most gullible people, and every scammer knows it. They all call you. Your entire life has been dictated by what other people convince you is true."

Thomas frowned. "No, I chose to come here because it sounded romantic. I liked the thought of you hanging on my arm, working our way through mysterious caves. I thought it would be fun. Something to rekindle what we used to have."

"Well, that's a little difficult when our relationship is based on me bailing you out whenever you get into trouble," she snapped, then removed herself to the opposite side of the cave.

Thomas released a long sigh. When his gaze found me,

I quickly looked away, embarrassed at being caught so blatantly eavesdropping.

"It's true," Thomas said, dropping to the cave floor. He pulled his knees into his chest, his gaze settling on where our path likely would have led if Ranger Eric hadn't met his early demise. "I'm a dreamer. And a sucker. The problem is that even though I know it, I can't for the life of me look a scammer in the face and realize they're lying to me. I believe most people are genuinely good. I believe in God and in miracles. I believe that anything is possible. And I'm terrified of missing an amazing opportunity because I was too cynical to see it. Or missing out on an amazing relationship because I assumed she was out of my league."

I walked over to Thomas and sat down next to him. "I think that's admirable."

Thomas hesitated. "Thank you for saying that, but no, I don't believe it is. Amber is right. It's gotten me into a lot of trouble in the past. And she has every right to be angry with me. To be honest, I don't know why she's stuck with me as long as she has." He glanced toward where Eric lay. "You're sure he's dead? And you really think someone killed him?"

I gave a small nod. "Yes. I do."

Thomas's gaze became guarded as he took in the people who surrounded us. Mr. Harding was now examining Ranger Eric, like he was a museum exhibit. Jasmine and Violet stood on the opposite side of the cave, Violet's arms wrapped around her sister. Amber seemed like she was more a woman of action, using her headlamp to examine the ground, like she might be able to help find us a way out of there.

And then there was my family.

Flash stood next to the body, his arms crossed, guarding it from anyone who thought they might disturb any evidence. Namely Mr. Harding. Lilly was next to Flash, looking at the pictures she'd taken on her camera.

Benji walked over to me, nodding to Thomas in greeting. "Can I talk to you for a moment?" he asked me, his voice low.

I excused myself, and we walked to the edge of the cave.

"We need to find out who knew Ranger Eric before coming on this tour," he told me, his tone urgent.

"That would be helpful," I said. "We figure out who killed him, then we can detain them until help arrives. There's no way we'll get Eric's body out of here on our own."

Benji wrung his hands and glanced back toward my kids, who were now talking with Mr. Harding. "That's not my biggest concern right now. No one here, other than Charlie, seemed to know Eric. All of us come from different parts of the country, here to experience the caverns. Why would anyone here want him dead?" He paused. "What if there really isn't any connection between Eric and the others on this tour?"

I quieted as my mind attempted to catch up. "You mean...what if this was a random killing? Someone takes out the only person who knows the path, leaving us stranded. Vulnerable." My breath caught in my throat as I began to understand what Benji was getting at. "You think they could strike again. That it wasn't personal. It was pleasure."

6

I took Benji's hands in mine, truly scared for the first time since we'd embarked on this tour. Even after discovering that Eric had been killed, I hadn't felt we were in danger. Murder was supposed to be emotional. Personal. And we didn't know anyone here.

But if this was premeditated, and there was no connection between Eric and the killer, we were dealing with someone who didn't care about emotion. They would have known there were only three Lower Cave tours a week. They had bought tickets. Targeted the guide so the rest of us couldn't leave. The murderer wouldn't have known who the participants would be, but that likely gave them a thrill.

I was thinking like my ex-husband now. He was an expert on serial killers—had even written books on the psychology of why they do what they do. I'd hated it.

And yet here we were.

"We should send a couple people back to retrace our steps," I said. "Do what Amber is doing—study the ground and follow our footprints. Those people can bring back help."

Benji pulled me into a tight hug, staying silent until my heartbeat slowed next to his chest. "We can't do that," he murmured against my hair. "First, what if they get lost? We'd be separated and worse off than when we started."

"And second?" I asked, scared to know the answer.

"What if one of the people we send back to get help is the murderer?"

Oh. That would be bad. But was it as bad as being stuck down here with them?

"So, what's the alternative?" I asked, feeling my anxiety rising and struggling to breathe.

Benji pulled back. "I don't like the idea of all of us wandering around in unfamiliar caves. We need to follow the same protocol as if we got lost hiking. Stay in one spot. Someone will notice when the rangers don't return for whatever tours or duties they have this afternoon. They'll come looking."

"And until then?" I asked.

Benji's gaze met mine. "We keep everyone safe."

Safe.

The only way I'd feel safe is if I had the murderer hogtied on the ground, ready to be delivered to the police.

Which meant that like it or not, I had a murder to solve.

I must have had a look on my face that gave away every thought that had just passed through, because Benji's lips dipped into a frown. "No. It's too dangerous. This is different than what you've done in the past. You've always had support from Sheriff Potts or other law enforcement. An escape route. We're too vulnerable here, and if the killer realizes what you're doing..."

He was right. I didn't know what I'd been thinking, especially with my kids here.

"Okay." My voice was small and weak. I hated feeling like we were just sitting around, hoping no one else would be picked off while we waited. But what other choice did we have?

At least, what other choice that wouldn't get someone else killed?

So I found a rock outcrop and sat on it. My gaze wandered. I hadn't intended to study each person and search their expressions for reactions to Ranger Eric being murdered.

My legs had merely been getting tired.

But as a psychologist by nature, I couldn't help it. Every day, everywhere I went, I was constantly observing people —wondering what life choices had led to them walking down a particular street at a particular time, and why had they chosen that particular outfit or shoe to wear?

Some people would find it exhausting, but I found it fascinating.

Now was no different.

Jasmine was sobbing at one end of the cavern, and I couldn't tell if it was out of fear or sadness. Violet had her hand on her sister's back, looking more exasperated than sad, and was murmuring something in Jasmine's ear. Maybe words of comfort?

If Ranger Eric had been the man Jasmine was here to confront, it was possible she had been able to say what she'd needed and her tears were ones of regret. Her last words to him would have been said out of anger. If she hadn't been able to speak with him, those tears would still be born of regret, as she'd wish she'd taken the chance to make amends when she'd had it.

Unless she was the murderer, of course, and had killed him out of anger, which once again would lead her to regret.

Maybe?

I shook my head. This not investigating a murder was not going very well.

My attention moved to the reporter, Mr. Harding. Even though my kids were still standing guard over Eric's body like sentries, making sure no one disturbed the evidence, he didn't seem to mind as he took pictures with his phone. He seemed more interested in the narrative than in the man himself. I supposed he saw dead bodies on a regular basis, a story already forming in his mind. This would be his lucky break—the one that would make him famous. Trapped in the Carlsbad Caverns with a body and a murderer on the loose. It didn't get better than that. If he survived to tell the story.

Thomas walked past Mr. Harding, clicking his tongue in disapproval. "Have you no respect for the dead?"

"Of course I do," Mr. Harding said, shooting Thomas a look of annoyance. "It would be disrespectful to not tell the story of Ranger Eric Lancaster, cut down in his prime. Everyone deserves to know who he is and why he was so savagely ripped from this Earth, a thousand feet underground, no less."

Thomas leaned forward. "It sounds like you're saying you know why our ranger was killed." His gaze was intense. "Do you know something the rest of us don't?"

Every head swiveled toward the bickering duo. Even Jasmine's sobs had quieted as we awaited the journalist's answer.

"Detecting is in my nature. It's what I do," Mr. Harding said, now carefully choosing each word. "I haven't discovered the 'why' yet, and without access to his friends and family, or even cell phone reception, for that matter, it won't come easily. But I am going to bring Eric justice."

I wished he wouldn't have said that. A figurative target had now been painted on Mr. Harding, and it seemed silly that my kids were protecting a dead body. It wasn't Eric who needed protection.

"You're saying you're going to solve the ranger's

murder?" Amber asked slowly. "Or does your version of justice actually mean pulling out all the skeletons from Eric's closet to give your story more juicy details?"

Mr. Harding held up a finger. "Facts give a story depth. For good or for bad."

Amber snorted and shook her head. "Justice, indeed."

My attention strayed when I heard muttering from the far right of us.

Ranger Charlie. I'd nearly forgotten about him.

He stood at the edge of the cavern. I pushed myself off my makeshift rock bench and walked toward him.

"They were here. I know they were," he was saying to himself while pacing back and forth, combing his fingers through his hair.

"Charlie?" I reached out a finger and lightly tapped him on the shoulder.

The boy shrieked, his screams echoing off the rock walls.

Everyone else whipped toward us, immediately on high alert, their expressions panicked, likely thinking we'd just had a second murder.

I gave an uneasy laugh and waved. "Nothing to see here. Just a case of the jitters."

No one looked like they bought it, and Benji was watching me with a concerned expression, likely thinking I was investigating something I had no business being involved in, but I gave him a look that was supposed to mean *trust me*, and I hoped he would.

I wasn't here to find a murderer, only help a young man who was clearly in need of some intervention.

"You okay, Charlie?" I asked. "This has to be the worst day on a job anyone has ever had."

Charlie's hands were shaking, and he shoved them in his pockets. "There was supposed to be tape lining the path to protect formations from being handled by the public. This type of tour allows you to get up close and personal, but the national park does have its limits. Can't have people wandering all over these caverns, posing on formations for pictures or—"

"Getting lost?" I guessed.

He nodded slowly. "It was all in the orientation. This tour has been closed for a few years, but they replaced all the old stuff. Eric brought me down here two nights ago and gave me the tour so I'd be at least somewhat acquainted with what we'd be doing today. The tape was here."

"So it wasn't that someone forgot," I said, more to myself than anyone else. "It was purposely removed. Which means that it had to be someone who knew this cavern."

"Not necessarily."

I glanced at him, my eyebrows dipping in confusion. "What do you mean?"

Charlie raised a shoulder. "Someone follows the path to a certain point, and then removes it as they return to the beginning."

Oh, that was diabolical. And could totally be what had happened.

"So, why didn't Eric stop the tour when he saw the missing tape? Surely that's a safety issue."

Charlie looked as lost as I felt as he struggled to find an answer. "He's been down here so many times, maybe the thought of angry guests was worse than taking a tour with missing tape. Eric has worked at the caverns for ten years —he wouldn't get lost."

Someone had removed the tape, knowing they would then kill the only guide that could lead everyone back to the top.

"This doesn't make sense," I said. When Charlie opened his mouth to protest, I waved a hand. "No, not what you said. I mean, the killer trapped themselves down here with everyone else. Even if they figured out the way back when they were down here removing the tape, they can't actually let on that they know the way out. If you're going to kill someone, there has to be easier ways. All of this—it's too theatrical. Too complicated. Why make things harder on yourself?"

Charlie thought on that a moment, and I realized I was doing it again. Benji had been right to be worried. I was investigating. And I had dragged Charlie into it with me.

7

"Forget I said anything," I said, backing away from Charlie. "Sometimes I have an overactive imagination. Half the time, I think I should have been an author, making up stories the way I do."

Charlie tried to stop me from retreating, and he stepped toward me. "It's not farfetched. If we're going to be trapped down here for a few more hours—and Eric's killer has the advantage of knowing the way out—we need to find him. Or her. Right?"

I gave a vigorous shake of my head. "No. We don't. It's too dangerous. I won't risk anyone's life like that. Including mine. I'm sorry, but we're going to need to sit tight and let the police handle it once we get out of here."

Charlie frowned. "Really? My mentor was killed, and we're just going to stare at him—like he's part of the landscape."

It did sound kind of awful when he said it like that.

"Would it help if I placed my sweater over him to give him some privacy?" My voice held no conviction. It sounded stupid in my head, even before I'd said it out loud. That only made it sound worse. I released a defeated sigh. "Fine. You're right. But what are we supposed to do about it? Even if we discovered who the killer was, that would only make them agitated and more likely to do something rash. That isn't going to help Eric, and it certainly won't help us."

Of course, Flash had to run up to me at that moment.

"We think we know who did it," he proudly proclaimed, loudly enough for all to hear.

Anxiety rushed through me as my mind worked at double speed, trying to figure out a way out of this. It was bad enough that Mr. Harding had a target on his back, but I refused to allow Flash to be in the killer's crosshairs too.

"You figured out who cheated on your final exam last semester?" I asked, my words equally loud but less convincing. "Maybe this is a conversation for after we get out of here." I hoped he got the hint.

He didn't.

Benji hurried over to offer a helping hand, but Flash's mouth was faster.

"What are you talking about? Someone cheated? That would be dumb. Graduation was a week away—why go to the trouble?"

Why go to the trouble indeed?

The only reason to murder someone a thousand feet underground would be if you didn't want anyone to discover the body, which obviously wasn't the case here. Unless you only wanted to keep specific people from finding the body too quickly. Maybe we didn't count.

I cursed my brain, begging it to shut off for just a moment so I could deal with the bigger problem at hand.

"You don't know who did it," I muttered to Flash. "And even if you do, you're going to keep it to yourself, do you understand me?"

He heard the urgency in my voice, but he didn't understand it. "Why? If we know who did it, we can make a citizen's arrest. She's outnumbered. It wouldn't take much to keep her in line."

That gave me pause. Before I could react, though, someone else did.

"She? It was a woman?"

I nearly jumped out of my skin, not realizing that Charlie had crept forward and was standing so close, his breath had tickled the hair on the back of my head, sending my heart racing.

"Charlie, you can't inject yourself into someone else's conversation like that," I said, my breaths coming hard.

"Even if it affects me?" he asked, frowning.

"I—maybe—yes. Even then." I took a couple of long pulls of air, then turned to Flash. "I'm begging you. Please don't say anything more. Not until we have law enforcement here."

Charlie placed himself between me and Flash, his voice eager. "We can take her down now. We're both young and strong. Jasmine, Violet, Amber—none of them are any match for us." His gaze was intense, like he was excited by the thought.

It made me uncomfortable.

"What does it matter if it's now or later?" I asked.

Benji rested a hand on my arm, reminding me of his presence. "Even if we don't take action now, it would be good to know who we are keeping an eye on," he said, his voice low.

I had been warned not to investigate—not to let anyone think we were trying to figure out who the murderer was. We had determined that it would put us in danger.

"I'm scared," I whispered back, my gaze taking in our dim surroundings. Our headlamps created shadows on the cavern walls. It made me wonder how Jim White had managed it a century earlier. He could have died down here, and no one would have been the wiser. There had been no tours. No one would have known where to come looking.

Benji pulled me into a side hug. "I know. But would you rather be blindly waiting, wondering who you can trust and who might stab you in the back? And I mean that quite literally."

I squeezed my eyes shut. "All right, Flash. What have you discovered?"

"It was Jasmine," Flash said, puffing his chest out. He had often assisted me in investigations I had unwittingly become a part of, but this was different. This was him taking charge.

"Jasmine?" I said, glancing over at the scared and timid woman who continued to put distance between herself and Ranger Eric. "Are you sure? The woman is terrified of...everything. I'm not sure she's capable."

Flash held up a finger. "It's always the quiet ones you have to look out for. All the pent-up rage they've been shoving down for so long. See, Jasmine might be quiet, but Violet didn't waste any time confronting her sister. They've been huddled together arguing for the past ten minutes about how they shouldn't have come and that Violet didn't know her sister was prepared to go so far with things. They forget how well sound travels in this place."

Benji and I shared looks. Mine was supposed to read, *what do you think we should do now?* But Benji's look must have meant something different because he gave a decided nod and then spun on his heel, walking quickly toward the two sisters, who had settled into an angry silence. Their fury toward each other radiated across the cavern, and I had no idea what Benji's plan was, but he had better hope that Jasmine didn't have another flashlight on her.

I followed at a distance, just in case.

"What a day, huh?" he asked when he reached them, shaking his head. "And to think this was supposed to be a family getaway to get Maddie's mind off the upcoming wedding. I suppose it worked, just not in the way we had hoped."

Violet glanced up at Benji but didn't say anything, likely trying to figure out why this guy was talking to them when they so clearly wanted to be left alone.

Jasmine was more open, surprisingly, and her gaze jumped from Benji to me in the background, then back to Benji. "Congratulations. If I were getting married, I'd not want to stop thinking about it ever."

"It's overrated," Violet said. Benji raised an eyebrow, and she added, "I'm divorced."

Jasmine frowned. "There's someone out there who's perfect for me. And we'll have the little cottage and the yard to take care of. I'll write for a living, as will he. He'll be a deep thinker, and we can take a break midday to exchange ideas. He'll love me for my mind." She stared into the distance wistfully, relishing the dream that had not yet been realized.

Violet released a sound of derision. "Pipe dreams. Considering you broke up with your cheating boyfriend only last week, I'm shocked you're still hanging on to that particular fantasy."

Before Jasmine had the chance to retort, Benji interjected. "We have some time on our hands, and in light of the recent events of our guide being killed and us getting trapped down here, Maddie has offered to do one-on-one sessions with anyone who would like it. Just a chance to try to process everything, you know. Trauma counseling."

Oh, that was what he'd thought my look had meant. That was actually pretty good. Better than anything I'd come up with. Which had been nothing.

Violet's gaze held suspicion. "I don't think we'd be interested in spilling our innermost thoughts to a complete stranger, but thanks anyway."

It seemed that Jasmine was more than happy to do just that. I took a tentative step forward. "We wouldn't need to talk about anything you didn't want to. But you've been through an intense situation, and it can help to speak to an outsider. Someone who doesn't have to go home with you at the end of the day. A lot of people find it cathartic being able to say whatever they want—an opportunity to be truly honest with no repercussions."

Jasmine's expression was the opposite of her sister's. She was open and eager, and I could see the yearning in her eyes. This was a woman who had a lot on her mind, and she wanted to be rid of it all. She wanted someone to finally listen to what she had to say, without risking the cold shoulder Violet was giving her.

"Maybe we could go around the corner into the next cavern," Jasmine said, standing. "It would provide a little more privacy but not be so far that we'd get lost."

I smiled and held out an arm. "That's a great idea. Lead the way."

8

Should I be valuing Jasmine's privacy when the second we turned a corner, she could murder me?

Probably not.

But the way sound echoed in the chamber, she wasn't going to say anything remotely useful if she thought we were being overheard.

When we turned the corner, I released a sharp gasp. Directly in front of us were two tall formations that looked like something that wanted to eat us, especially with the light from our headlamps bouncing around. I gave a nervous laugh, hoping Jasmine hadn't noticed.

I averted my eyes from the formations and found a flatish rock that would work for our purposes. As I sat down, the cold immediately penetrated my pants, but I ignored it and patted the spot next to me.

"I have to say," I started as she took a seat, "I'm

surprised to see you on this tour. I was in the visitor's center yesterday when you were struggling with your fear of the dark."

Jasmine looked down at her hands. "When you say it like that, it makes me sound like a small child who still sleeps with their nightlight on."

She was obviously embarrassed by this, and I started to apologize, because that certainly hadn't been my intention, but she stopped me.

"You don't need to be sorry. Your job is to get me to be honest, right? And the truth is that I do still sleep with a nightlight. It's not the dark, necessarily, that scares me. It's what comes out of it. The shadows. Never knowing what's lurking or what I can't see. The dark—it distorts everything."

Wow, Jasmine was jumping in with both feet. She was braver than she let on.

"It sounds like something has come out of the dark before," I said, my voice soft. Everything sounded louder in the cavern. Like it was holding its breath and the tiniest whisper became a roar.

Jasmine gave a small nod. "My life has been nothing but shadows. My parents fought constantly when I was young. Violet and I always hid in our bedroom, waiting for it to be over. We never knew if it would be our mother or father who would come into our bedroom when it was all over. Always terrified it would be the latter. It wasn't until I was a teenager that our mom finally kicked our dad out of the house. It took too long, but at least she finally managed it. She had to save enough money, you see. Some way to support us."

The picture-perfect marriage Jasmine fantasized about was starting to make sense.

"So, you're a writer. Someone who can support yourself," I said. "And you've created an image of a lovely man who shares a lovely home with you, and no one yells or abuses the other."

Jasmine's gaze met mine. "Violet says it's a fantasy and that I need to wake up. The world isn't as good as all that. Her point was proven when I caught...a former boyfriend...cheating on me. I'd built him up as this wonderful person and ignored all the warning signs. The worst part was dealing with Violet saying *I told you so*. Yes, she was right. I was wrong. The world is a cruel place. That doesn't mean she has to kick me while I'm down."

"That must have been traumatic. How did you and your boyfriend meet?" I studied Jasmine's expression as she searched for the right answer.

"Online," she finally admitted. That must have made it easier for her to construct her fantasy. Without having to see someone in real life, he could be anyone she wanted him to be, and vice versa. All he had to do was say the right words, and she'd do anything for him.

"It was devastating," Jasmine said. She hesitated, then plunged forward. "It all seems so silly now, because I never actually met him in person. We messaged each other on social media for years, exchanging pictures. But I never actually had the opportunity to make sure he was who he said he was. Violet said that was a bad sign, that I was something to play with—a source of entertainment—but here I was planning our cottage and garden in some nonexistent field of flowers. I mean, when I look at myself in the mirror, I can't believe what a sucker I've been."

I held up a finger. "I'm going to stop you right there. You need to be kinder to yourself. You suffered a lot of trauma as a child. A lot of uncertainty and misdirected anger and abuse. Believing in the good in people has been your coping strategy. You have this need to believe, even though all evidence points to the world being a terrible, scary place, that there is someplace that is safe. Someplace you can hide from all the evil that lives around us. The shadows. The dark. All you want is light. And someone who loves you and will keep you in that safe place. That isn't a bad thing. The key is distinguishing the dark from the light and knowing that sometimes a little fog sneaks in."

Jasmine buried her head in her hands and was quiet for a moment. I let her take all the time she needed. I doubted she'd ever visited a therapist before, and she desperately needed it. "I always told myself that if I had been my mom, I would have left my dad the moment he mistreated me." She looked up. "So when I found out that my boyfriend had a girlfriend, and it wasn't me, I had to come here. Confront him." She paused, realizing she'd said too much, and she searched my expression. When I didn't say anything but merely nodded, she stared, incredulous. "You don't seem surprised."

I decided to leave Flash out of it. I didn't know how much he'd overheard, and considering Jasmine and I were secluded away from everyone else, I didn't want to dive in without knowing how deep the water was. "Yesterday, my family did the self-guided tour," I said. "I overheard you in the bathroom saying you needed to face your fears and confront a man. No one has shown evidence they know you on this tour, but it makes sense now that I know you two had never met in person. That's why he didn't recognize you. When we meet someone in a situation we don't expect them to be in, we often don't piece the puzzle together. Our brain doesn't see it as even a possibility."

Moisture filled Jasmine's eyes. "But two years. And nothing. I've sent him pictures of me at every vacation I've taken, at a writer's convention, even a picture of me right after surgery. Everything. And he didn't have the foggiest idea who I was."

This was a heartbroken woman. But murderous? I wasn't so sure.

"You must have been furious. I know I would have confronted him right then and there. Made him realize who I was and what he'd done to me."

She released a humorless laugh. "Oh, trust me, I wanted to. But it didn't feel like the right moment. He could have easily dismissed me. Walked away. And I fully expected him to."

"So, you booked this tour. One where you knew he'd be stuck with you for three hours. Underground. Nowhere to escape what he'd done."

Jasmine released a shuddered breath. "You were right before. Telling you all of this... It feels like I've released a toxin that's been eating me from the inside out. And to be able to do so with no judgment from you—it's amazing. Do you do long-distance sessions? Because I could really use someone like you on my team."

I laughed. "We might be able to work something out, though I'm certain you have someone just as good—if not better—that's more local to you." I started to stand but then stopped. I hadn't asked the hardest question, but I wondered if I needed to. Even if Jasmine had killed Eric, it would have been a crime of passion. The rest of us weren't in danger.

The problem was, what if she hadn't killed him?

Then we weren't any better off than we had been. Not that I wanted Jasmine to be guilty—I really liked the woman. But the alternative scared me.

"Jasmine, I hate to ask. Have you had the chance to confront this man about what he's done to you?"

She stood, wiping her eyes, and a little smile peeked through the sadness, like the question amused her. She shook her head. "I had a chance. But even though I'd run through what I'd say to him a million times, when the moment came, I lost my nerve. I stared at the back of his head as we walked, anger building within me because the man I thought I'd loved didn't know me from just another tourist. But I couldn't bring myself to say anything. I've always judged my mom so harshly for not leaving my dad earlier. I'd thought her a coward. I was wrong."

"Coming here at all took bravery," I said.

Jasmine stepped past me toward the main cavern. "Maybe." She glanced over her shoulder at me. "But in the end, it doesn't matter. Because I'm not the only one he's betrayed. It doesn't have to be me who confronts him or takes care of the problem. There will always be someone else."

And then she walked away.

It wasn't exactly a confession, but unless I was mistaken, Jasmine hadn't been crying because Eric was dead. She was upset she hadn't had the guts to do it first.

9

Flash and Lilly were at my side the moment I reappeared in the cavern. Lilly's expression was one of worry, and Flash's was one of excitement. No surprise there.

"Well?" he asked. "Did you get her to confess? Is there a dungeon-like cavern we can keep her in until someone realizes we're missing and rescues us?"

"Flash, you dummy, *we* are in the dungeon," Lilly said. "This entire place belongs under a castle, skeletons hung by their wrists in the corners, warning people of what's to come. We even have the dead body to prove it."

She wasn't wrong.

I placed a hand on Flash's shoulder, hoping it would help calm him. "You have to keep your voice down, because I'm not sure she did it, and spreading rumors in this type of situation is only going to lead to trouble."

That was enough to bring his energy down. His shoulders drooped, and he gave a little shrug. "Oh. Okay. So...I wasn't helpful?"

I hated to see his smile replaced by disappointment. Flash had been so excited because he'd thought he'd helped catch a killer. That he'd finally been the one to solve the case.

"It was immensely helpful," I said. "Because of you, we have more information than we had before, and we have a window into what kind of man Eric was. Just because we don't know who hurt him doesn't mean you didn't do a good job."

Great, now I was reassuring my son that he had done a good job trying to catch a killer. Did other moms have to deal with this sort of thing?

"You can say the M word," Lilly said. "We've done this enough times, and we're old enough to know someone didn't hurt him. They murdered him. And then you went off on your own for a therapy session, to a secluded area, where you could have met with the same fate." She raised an eyebrow, like I should have known better.

The older my kids got, the more I felt like they were more the parent in our relationship than I was.

And then I glanced at Flash, who was doing shadow puppets with his hands on the walls.

That made me feel better.

Benji walked up and wrapped an arm around my waist.

"You okay?" he whispered in my ear. "We were worried, and I realized that was a terrible plan. I put you in danger."

I turned and wrapped my arms around his neck. "It was actually a brilliant plan. The dangerous part was on me—I shouldn't have suggested leaving the group like that."

Benji's eyebrow cocked. "You didn't. It was Jasmine who suggested it."

Had it been?

Oh my gosh, it had. That was a really scary thought.

"It made sense at the time," I said. "People want privacy if they're going to talk about their innermost thoughts."

"That's true," Benji agreed. "But in this type of situation, no one else gets that luxury. You are not leaving my sight."

I smiled and gave him a quick kiss. "I'm okay with that. But I doubt there will be any other therapy sessions. I was only testing out Flash's theory, and now we have a little more information on Jasmine's traumatic childhood and what a jerk Eric was. But I'm no more convinced of Jasmine's guilt or innocence than I was thirty minutes ago."

Benji's eyebrows scrunched up, and I recognized it as his own look of guilt.

"What did you do?"

There wasn't a need for Benji to answer my question because Thomas approached us at that moment, his eyes lit up in excitement. "I've never had a therapy appointment before. Is it like in the movies, where you look into my soul and interpret my dreams, leading me on the road to recovery and self-actualization?"

Benji avoided my gaze and attempted to hide a smile, as I tried to not look frustrated with my husband-to-be. He had obviously assumed I wanted to have a therapy session with everyone stuck in this cavern. After all, it wasn't every day you were trapped with a dead body while waiting for someone to rescue you.

I turned a smile on Thomas. "This is more to help you not be traumatized by current events. The film industry tends to exaggerate both the positives and negatives of receiving therapy. I hope this time together does help, but I can't guarantee it will change your life."

My words didn't seem to faze him.

"Sounds good to me. Same place you had your session with Jasmine?" He didn't wait for an answer, trotting ahead and around the corner I'd just reemerged from.

"Actually, Thomas," I said, speed-walking after him. "I was thinking we could do it out here, you know, so we aren't so removed from the rest of the group. Benji worries, you know."

Thomas nodded in understanding, retaining his eager smile. "He's worried I'll try to make a move on you. Trapped in an underground cavern can be quite romantic, and then us secluded away from the others—I get it."

I blinked. "Uh, no. That's not it. It's because our guide was murdered. And you know...the murderer..."

"Is still with us." Thomas finished my sentence with a solemn nod. "He's afraid I'm the murderer, and then it will be all Stockholm syndrome and you'll fall in love with me before becoming my accomplice. Even though I've never done therapy, I do know a little bit about psychology. It's an unlikely scenario—I've never killed anyone before—but I suppose your fiancé doesn't know that. If it makes him more comfortable being able to see you at all times, because you know, he doesn't trust you, then sure, we can rejoin the others. Of course, then I won't be able to be truly open about my feelings because I'll be afraid that others will be listening in, and I don't think I'll derive the same benefit from a therapy session that Jasmine did, but you have to do you. I get it."

My head was spinning, unsure how we had gotten from point A to point B, then circled around, done a roller-coaster, and ended up at point Z. Someplace I hadn't even known existed and didn't recognize.

"Um..." It was a lose-lose situation. Either Thomas didn't feel valued and this was a waste of our time because he'd spend the entire time watching his words, afraid of his girlfriend overhearing, or I'd have a fruitful session but be at risk of dying at the hands of a gullible murderer.

Of course, everyone knew I was with him. He'd have to be crazy to think he could kill me and people wouldn't realize it was him.

I was counting on him not being crazy.

"You know what," I finally said. "You're right. You

shouldn't feel worried that the others will hear and judge the things you have to say. You should be able to cry, if you feel the need, and admit your unwanted fears or desires, all without repercussions."

Thomas grinned as he walked around the corner and then sat where Jasmine had been a few minutes earlier. "I know Benji is worried, but I want to assure you I'm not going to fall in love with you. I know that a lot of patients do develop feelings for their therapist, because they are one of the few people in their lives that listen to them and seem to genuinely care. The patients share their innermost thoughts and deepest feelings with their therapist, and that's an intense connection. But I am in love with Amber."

I wondered if I had inadvertently done something to send Thomas signals, because he was struggling to move past this topic. I thought back to the past hour but couldn't think of anything. I'd been nice to him, but in a purely distant, platonic, acquaintance kind of way. Maybe Thomas wasn't used to people being nice to him.

"Thank you for the heads up," I finally said. "For a therapist to become involved with one of their patients would be deeply unethical. I could lose my license, and my business. All that to say, I agree with you, and my only desire is to help you."

Thomas steepled his fingers under his chin. "Although, a forbidden love in an underground cavern is quite exciting, isn't it?"

I stared, confused about what was happening. Thomas

had a way of twisting and turning things so I no longer knew which way was up or down.

The time for decorum had passed.

I threw my arms into the air in frustration. "Thomas, why do you think anything romantic could happen between us? You are dating Amber, and you said you love her. You seem to enjoy her company, so what's the problem?"

Thomas pointed at me. "You said I seem to enjoy her company. The same could be said about my co-workers or my dog. It's not something you say about a romantic partner. Yes, we fell in love. But now, she acts like she can barely stand the sight of me."

I thought back to when they'd first entered the orientation room and Amber had avoided holding his hand.

"How long have you two been dating?" I asked, sitting next to him but with enough distance between us that he couldn't get any wrong ideas about what was happening here. I leaned forward and rested my elbows on my knees. People wanted to feel that you were really listening, not just pretending, and maintaining eye contact was a great way to do that. My gaze never wavered.

I could immediately see Thomas's body language loosen, and his arms unfolded. "A year. We met at a concert at a small bar by my work. It was love at first sight. In fact, she's the one who approached me."

"You've been together ever since?"

Thomas nodded. "She slept over at my place that night.

I thought she'd wake up and realize it had all been one big mistake—that she was out of my league. But she didn't run or even walk away. Instead, we started seeing each other every evening. We'd meet up at the same bar after work, and she'd always come home with me. We'd talk for hours into the night. On the weekends, we'd go to all the local museums and parks. Couldn't get enough of each other."

The flame that burned the brightest at the beginning tended to burn out the fastest. I didn't know if that was actually how fire worked in the real world, but I'd seen it over and over in regard to relationships.

"When did it start to change?" I asked Thomas.

"A few months ago," he said. "She was late to our meet-up and looked flushed. Like she'd been running."

I knew exactly where his mind was going and tried to steer him away from it. "How long ago did you plan this trip to Carlsbad Caverns?"

"Four weeks ago. Some guys at work were talking about how awesome it was, and I told her we should come."

By this point I'd already be scribbling in my notebook that I kept locked up in my office. My fingers itched to at least hold a pen. Instead, I had to settle for clasping my hands together.

"Would she have agreed to come if she didn't want to spend the time with you?"

"Probably," Thomas said, raising a shoulder. "She's not very good at expressing her feelings, so I have to guess at what she's thinking most of the time. Doesn't like confrontation, and that kind of thing. Maybe I should be grateful for it. If she was better at it, she'd probably have broken up with me weeks ago."

That was a distinct possibility. As gullible and silly as Thomas seemed most of the time, I saw intelligence lurking beneath the facade.

"You've mentioned your job a few times," I said, attempting a smooth segue. "What do you do for work?"

Thomas hesitated, his guard suddenly up, and his gaze bounced around the dark passageway. "I work for a jeweler as a gemologist."

That made sense to me—I'd expected something that didn't offer a lot of social interaction. Many people likely entered the jewelry store, but Thomas would be tucked away in the back, alone.

Maybe that was why Amber had been dating Thomas. It was possible there was a lot of money to be made in the business of gemology, and it wasn't likely he'd meet another woman doing what he did, so she wouldn't have to worry about him cheating on her.

"What does a gemologist do?" I asked, hoping I sounded like I had only a passing interest.

It wasn't enough. Thomas's agitation increased, though he was trying desperately to keep it hidden. "I fix customers' jewelry and recut the gems when needed, sign certificates of authenticity, that sort of thing." He said it as if it were boring and like he expected I would be unimpressed with his routine. His body language said otherwise.

"Thomas, I can't help but notice you seem a little antsy. Does your job cause friction in your relationship?"

He hesitated once more but then nodded. "She used to ask about my job constantly and seemed genuinely interested in what I do. She'd ask how I can tell the difference between a real ruby and a fake one—that sort of thing. But lately she seems almost annoyed whenever I bring work up, even when it's just recounting a humorous story about something that happened with one of my co-workers. She even suggested that maybe I was meant for bigger and better things...like working for a jeweler is beneath me.

"If you ask me, it's beneath *her*. I don't make the money she wishes I did. When she says I should start looking for a different job, she says it like she's only looking out for my best interest. But I'm not stupid. I see it for what it is. She's embarrassed by me. It's the only thing that can explain why she comes with me to Sunday dinner at my parents' house each week, but when the opportunity arose to meet her family in California, she came up with a lame excuse about why it wouldn't work out, and maybe next time. When I suggest we do a video call with them, she avoids that too. To be honest, I don't think they even know about me."

One year of dating didn't seem very long to me, but considering she'd met Thomas's family and eaten dinner with them every week, something did seem off.

"Have you considered breaking up with her?" I asked, thinking of his overt innuendos that something could happen between me and him, thinly disguised as him shunning the idea. He was desperate for connection. To feel loved. And he was grasping for it wherever he could find it.

Thomas looked shocked and offended at the idea of breaking up with Amber. "Of course not. I love Amber. And this trip will help her to remember she loves me too."

"The dead body doesn't really help, does it?" I said, wondering if Ranger Eric's murder had even fazed him.

"No, it doesn't," he admitted. "And frankly, the caverns really aren't Amber's kind of thing. But it was something neither of us had done before, and you remember I'm getting my degree in geology. Being down here—I thought if she could see me in my element, rather than just a stuffy old jewelry store, that it would rekindle something in her. That my excitement would be contagious."

"What does Amber think about being trapped down here?" I asked. "You seem to be handling it pretty well."

Thomas's expression darkened for a brief second, and then it was gone, and his smile was back. "It has affected me, but I have to be strong for Amber, you know."

"What does she think about all this?" I repeated.

Thomas stared at me as if I had asked him a trick question. "I don't know," he admitted. "I can't imagine she likes it."

"You haven't asked her?"

He shook his head.

"What about all those museums and parks you visit on the weekends. Does she like those?"

Thomas was beginning to look uncomfortable. Good. I was finally getting under his skin. This was where he could start truly being honest. "I never asked. I assumed she'd say something if she didn't want to go."

"But you just told me that she avoids confrontation. Why would you assume she'd say anything if she didn't want to be there?"

Discomfort was giving way to anger. Thomas's expression twisted, his eyebrows dipping and his lips pursed. "I think this was a mistake," he said, standing.

Interesting. Thomas was all smiles until someone told him he was in the wrong. That his failed relationship was his fault.

Who was Thomas and why had he even volunteered for this impromptu therapy session? He obviously had no desire to actually work through real feelings. Everything was a front for him. Much like the glass gems he no doubt worked with, he had gotten very good at pretending to be something he wasn't.

What had Amber seen in him that he hadn't wanted her to?

Maybe she'd discovered the real Thomas, and that was why she had distanced herself.

I was suddenly afraid for her. And me.

10

————

I jumped to my feet and backed up toward the main cavern. "I'm sorry I couldn't be more help. Therapy isn't for everyone, and even for those it benefits, it can sometimes take months to chip away at our old beliefs and thought patterns."

I forced my feet to move slowly and steadily, not wanting them to mirror the panic in my heart. Turning my back on Thomas so I could move more quickly seemed like a bad idea, but the ground wasn't even, rocks protruding upwards at random places. So I kept my smile as I walked and hoped it would be enough to get to safety.

Benji had been right. I shouldn't be alone with anyone, no matter how harmless they seemed.

Even with my smile, Thomas must have sensed my fear.

His expression fell, and he slumped back onto the rock.

"I'm sorry," he said, his gaze fixed firmly on the ground. "I've scared you. Honestly, sometimes I scare myself. I'm a fake. A fraud. Willing to believe anything that anyone tells me, then turn around and do the same to others." He paused. "I lied before. I make plenty of money. People assume that if they throw enough of it at me, I'll overlook flaws in gems, or pretend I don't realize what they've handed me is a very impressive fake. The money doesn't tempt me. But their threats do make an impression. Especially when I know they'll follow through with them.

"I thought getting my gemology certification would open more career options for me. I was tired of hiking around in the dirt, and I was rethinking my degree. If I could get paid just as much to sit in an air-conditioned office and look at precious gems all day, there's no downside, right?" He released a long sigh and shook his head. "Amber looks at me and sees a weak man. Someone who is easily tricked into falling for one scam after another. That's mostly true. But what she doesn't realize is that the people I deal with on a daily basis—they aren't as sneaky as all that."

I nodded in understanding. "They bully you into doing what they need." My voice was quiet. I took a step back toward Thomas, feeling sorry for him. His previous anger hadn't been directed at me. It had been directed at himself. "When you received your certification, it meant you became the guy people went to for authentication, whether the gems were truly authentic or not."

The edge of Thomas's lips pulled up, as if he found the idea funny. "I was hired to work at this jewelry store without even an interview, likely because I was seen as someone who was gullible and would sign anything that was placed in front of me. They didn't count on my eye for detail. Yes, I am easily tricked. But not by my eyes—not by something tangible that I can hold in my hands. I can identify fake gems in half the time of other gemologists. It doesn't matter how professionally it has been done. You'd think that would be a good thing. And if I worked in a legitimate auction house or somewhere similar, it would be. There are people willing to pay a lot of money for my skills."

He fell silent, and I waited for him to continue.

Instead, he found his footing, stood up for a second time, and held out his hand. I shook it.

He didn't let go. "Thank you," he said. "For everything. I've been trying so hard with Amber, convinced that the problems in our relationship had everything to do with her. They don't. If I were her, I wouldn't want to be with me either. She should leave me. She won't, of course, because she's too nice for that. It doesn't matter what I've done, these past few months she's always stood by my side. Sometimes with a stern expression and a sad shake of her head, but she's always been there. Which means that I'm going to have to be the one to do it. I'm going to break up with her."

And then he walked past me, his shoulders squared

and confident.

"You're going to do it right now?" I asked, hurrying after him. "Are you sure that's a wise idea?" His footsteps didn't slow. "Have you ever broken up with someone before? It's usually quite awkward after, and she won't be able to leave. Neither will you. Trapped underground with a dead body. There has to be a better time. Maybe choose a nice restaurant once we're out of here."

Thomas glanced back over his shoulder. "I've been a burden long enough. No point in delaying the inevitable. Why should Amber suffer for my life choices? It's not fair."

And then he entered the cavern. It was silent, everyone sitting in their separate spaces. I could feel the tension and restlessness that permeated the room. They didn't trust each other, for good reason, and they didn't know how long they'd all be trapped together. The only one trying to help lift people's spirits was Ranger Charlie. Maybe he thought it was his duty, considering he was the only employee on hand. Even though he didn't know much more about the tour than we did, that didn't stop him from attempting to instill hope in the visitors.

"Cheer up. It's not all that bad," Charlie said with a large grin. "What if we played the question game? Each person takes a turn asking a question, and we all have to answer it." He held up a finger. "The only catch is that the person who asks the question always has to answer it, so don't go asking anything embarrassing if you're not willing to answer it yourself."

"It's a pointless game," Violet said. "People lie."

Charlie's lips parted, like he hadn't even considered that as a possibility. "Surely we wouldn't. I mean, we're stuck together in an underground cavern. That's the type of thing that brings people together—bonds them."

Jasmine sadly shook her head. "Yes, but one of us is a murderer, right? I doubt that person would have the motivation to be honest. And then it would turn into a different game. Two truths and a lie. We'd all be wondering which one of us was pretending. Which one of us is capable of smashing in another person's skull, leaving themselves trapped with the rest of us. Unless..." Jasmine's eyes widened. "The murderer knows how to get out of here. They're just pretending to be trapped. We could have escaped an hour ago, but they can't let on that they know how to leave."

And that was the moment Thomas decided to make his declaration.

"I'm breaking up with you, Amber," he announced loudly, the words bursting from his lips like he couldn't contain them a moment longer. "I love you, but I know you don't love me in return. You tolerate me. And I get it. I'm a difficult person to live with. I sign up for every free trial and then forget to cancel them. I respond to emails that ask for my personal information when I shouldn't. And I put my job above our relationship. I don't want to— I never meant for it to be like that. But what's done is done, and I can't change things. So, it's better that I free you and allow you to find someone who is worthy of your love."

Everyone stared at Thomas, their expressions mirroring the shock I felt. Even though I'd known it was coming, it was still difficult to hear the words said so forcefully at such an inopportune time, echoing off the rock around us.

"I'm sorry?" Amber said, springing to her feet.

Mr. Harding stepped in front of Thomas as Amber made a beeline toward him. "Let's everyone take a deep breath and calm down. Emotions are running high, and I'm sure Thomas didn't mean it. He just needs some fresh air." He clasped Thomas's arm and met his gaze. "Right?"

Amber didn't wait for Thomas's response, instead pushing Mr. Harding aside. "Thomas never says anything he doesn't mean. He's honest to a fault, which means that he is deadly serious right now." She winced at her poor choice of words. Taking Thomas's hands in hers, she moved in close. "You don't get to break up with me. Have I been conflicted about my feelings regarding our relationship? Yes. But that doesn't mean I want it to end. And certainly not down here. In front of everyone. If we never make it out of here, do you honestly want that to be the last thing you did—break someone's heart?"

Thomas's eyebrows scrunched in confusion. "I thought you'd find it to be a relief."

"You thought wrong." And then Amber wrapped him in a hug.

Jasmine dabbed at her eyes. "Oh, that's so sweet." She stood. "I'm sorry I thought you two could be the killers. I'd love to play the question game and get to know you better."

She approached the couple as they separated, still holding hands, and chatted with them like they'd been friends for years. I stared in awe as one by one, each of the members of our tour group, including my children, ended up walking over and sharing hugs. Like they needed to know they were there for each other. Tears were shed, likely the byproduct of the intense amount of anxiety we all shared, and then they all laughed when they realized how ridiculous they looked.

Benji came up to me. "What is happening here?" he whispered. "Did they forget that one of them is a murderer? Thomas and Amber's reconciliation doesn't change that."

"I..." I was trying to find words that I didn't have, because even I couldn't explain it, but I was cut off when Thomas collapsed onto the floor.

Amber screamed, and everyone else scattered to the far reaches of the cavern. It was akin to when lights turn on and cockroaches scatter to avoid being detected.

"He's dead," Amber said through a gasp, her finger on Thomas's neck as she frantically searched for a pulse, hoping to prove herself wrong.

Unfortunately, she was unable to do that.

We now had two dead bodies.

11

B enji and I rushed forward and knelt next to Amber, with my children cautiously approaching from behind.

"I was standing right next to Thomas," Flash said, pointing to an empty space. "He was there, with Amber, and then he just fell over. For no reason."

And yet Thomas was dead. How was that possible? Everyone had been standing there with him. They would have seen if someone had attacked him.

"Did he have a heart condition?" I asked Amber. "Something that could have been triggered by all the stress."

Even as I asked it, I knew what her answer would be. A second death within ninety minutes was too much of a coincidence.

"Nothing," Amber said. "He went to the gym every day after work, usually not getting home until eleven o'clock."

My first impression of Thomas had not been of an athletic man. His arms were too scrawny, his shoulders narrow. He didn't necessarily have to be big, but if he had been working out as much as Amber said he had, I would have expected at least some definition on the man.

"Okay, not a heart problem," I said slowly. "Of course, I'm no doctor, but..."

Amber stood. "You're thinking he was murdered. That our killer has struck again."

She didn't bother to lower her voice, her gaze landing on Jasmine and Violet.

"You think we had something to do with this?" Violet asked, her pitch rising. "Why would we want Thomas dead? We didn't even know him."

"No, you didn't," Amber said, her tone thoughtful. She was much too calm for the situation. Her boyfriend had just been murdered after they'd publicly declared their love for each other. But there were no tears. I could sense her sadness and disappointment—she wasn't by any means happy about this turn of events. But I'd expected more from her.

And there was another thing lurking beyond the sadness.

Calculation.

Rather than allowing herself to get upset, she was already trying to figure out who had done it.

"But Jasmine certainly has motive," Amber said, her words slow. When Jasmine opened her mouth to protest, Amber waved a hand through the air. "Don't bother. I overheard what happened to you. Your boyfriend cheated, right? Maybe you're on a vigilante mission to rid the world of stupid men."

Flash raised his hand, and I wanted to tell him to lower it—that he didn't want to be in the middle of this fight—but that would have only drawn more attention to him. Maybe they wouldn't notice.

Amber did notice, though, and she rolled her eyes in exasperation. "No, Flash, you don't count as one of the stupid men. You're too young to know any better."

"No, that's not it," he said. "I was just going to say that I don't think Jasmine murdered them. I'm more inclined to think it was you, or Violet, or maybe the reporter. I've always thought people in journalism had questionable ethics."

"Interesting," Amber said, sounding amused. Why wasn't she mad when she'd just been accused of murder?

Lilly pulled her brother back and placed him behind Benji as a sort of human shield, as if Amber had reacted to the accusation. Maybe Lilly had seen something I hadn't—something simmering. "Way to accuse the grieving girlfriend," she said. "Amber was wrong. You aren't too young to know any better—you really are just one of the stupid boys."

"Stupid men," Flash corrected her.

Oh, boy.

I glanced at Mr. Harding, worried about his reaction to Flash's insinuations, but he also didn't seem angry. On the contrary, he looked bored. And I noticed he had his phone out. He wasn't only recording this, he was taking a video.

"Mr. Harding," I said, approaching him. "These unfortunate events are not for your entertainment or for your article. You are currently trapped underground and are a murder suspect, as is everyone who is still alive. So please preserve the dignity of these two unfortunate men and put your phone away. You're worse than my two"—I almost said teenagers, not used to the fact that both were now grown— "children."

Lilly didn't like that term any better. "You make it sound like we're twelve."

I turned to her. "Well, what term would you use?"

She stayed silent for a moment, apparently unable to come up with anything better. "I wouldn't reference us at all. We don't need to be the examples in this situation."

"Regardless," I said, turning back to Mr. Harding, "my son has every right to suspect you. You're always on the outside of the group, until you weirdly joined everyone in that group hug...thing...and that really isn't your style, is it, Mr. Harding? Feel the need to get up close and personal with Thomas?"

Mr. Harding's eyes narrowed. "I already was up close and personal as I stood between Thomas and Amber. If you'll remember, I was protecting him. Why would I then turn around and kill him?"

"That's exactly what I would like to know," I said. But I knew Mr. Harding had made a good point. Was a newspaper article really motivation enough to kill two people? Maybe he'd thought it would make the story more interesting and get him a promotion. Maybe an award for being at the front line of all the drama. But that didn't seem like enough.

The problem was that we still had no idea how Thomas had even died.

We'd been able to find the murder weapon for Ranger Eric, and even though it hadn't helped us discover who the murderer was, maybe they'd slipped up by dropping another body. This was another chance to find evidence.

And we did need to find the murderer. We couldn't allow him, or her, to strike again.

"Empty your pockets," I said to Mr. Harding. "Both of them."

"But..."

"Now."

I wasn't one to command attention and expect people to do what I asked of them. I generally had a softer approach that coaxed people to think through their decisions and come to the realization that the desired action was in their best interest. But we didn't have time for that, and I doubted it would even work on the journalist.

Surprisingly, Mr. Harding did as I asked. It turned out

he had three pennies, a pack of gum, and a wallet in his pockets. Nothing that screamed murderer.

"Satisfied?" he asked me, clearly annoyed that I'd treated him in such a manner.

"For now," I said, allowing my gaze to stay on him long enough to make him uncomfortable. I didn't want him to think he was off the hook quite yet. Had to keep these people on their toes.

I turned to the rest of the room. "We're all emptying our pockets right now," I said in my mom voice. The one that said I meant business.

"I don't have pockets," Violet said, her tone smug. Apparently, she didn't like being told what to do. I didn't blame her.

I walked slowly toward her as the others turned out their pockets. "You have a jacket, don't you?" It was just now that I realized that hers was more of a half-jacket, something you'd likely see on a runway, and it had not been made for functionality.

Violet met my gaze and didn't turn away. "What I'm more interested in is what is in *your* pockets. Why are you the interrogator, when you are just as likely to be the killer as the rest of us? Maybe it's a family affair, and your fiancé, if that's who he really is, and your children are all in on it. Might give you a thrill, seeing your family come together for such a gruesome state of affairs."

"We only investigate murders, we don't commit them," Flash piped up. "Did you know we were there when a famous actor died? Lilly got his autograph right before he was murdered. Talk about crazy, right? He wasn't a bad guy, in case you were wondering. It was just a wrong time, wrong place type of situation."

I threw a panicked look at Lilly, and she clamped a hand over her brother's mouth, whispering in his ear as she did so. Likely telling him to knock it off. He may have graduated high school, but he still had zero impulse control. I wondered if it was premature allowing him to move out on his own in the next few months. He'd graduated early because he'd said he was too intelligent and the other kids at school were keeping him from fulfilling his true potential.

That may have been a mistake.

Violet cocked an eyebrow, her smugness morphing into pure delight. It was annoying when people thought they were right.

"So, you do this often?" she asked. "I'm sure I'm not alone when I say turn out your pockets. And your backpack."

Jasmine gave me an apologetic smile. "I think you should do as she asks."

Amber and Mr. Harding both nodded in agreement.

"Fine," I said. "You're right. My family shouldn't be exempt." I stuck my hands in my pockets and pulled them until they were inside out. I did the same with the backpack.

There was nothing to show except the water bladder

that was connected to my drinking tube. I had been grossly unprepared for this adventure, and had I thought about it further, I would have at least included a pair of hand warmers and some Chapstick.

"Happy?" I asked.

Violet's smile widened. "Very."

I didn't understand what she was so happy about until I realized she wasn't looking at me. She was looking at Flash. And in his hand was a syringe.

12

Flash's eyes widened, and his gaze whipped to me. "I swear, this isn't mine."

"Of course it's not," I said. "Where would you get a syringe, and what would you even do with one?"

Amber jumped toward Flash but then stopped, keeping her distance. As if my seventeen-year-old son was going to attack her if she got too close. "You killed Thomas," she said, her voice hoarse. It grew in intensity, and anger, as she repeated, "You killed Thomas."

Flash dropped the syringe on the ground. "I didn't, I swear. I've never killed anything, except a couple of centipedes. Some ants. A few flies—that's a lie. A ton of flies. Like, I can't even count how many flies I've killed over the years." A pause. "I sat on a dog once, but it survived. And that was absolutely not my fault. It's dangerous to breed dogs that small."

Oh my dear Lord, that boy needed to stop talking. The problem was that when he was nervous, it only got worse.

"My son didn't kill Ranger Eric or Thomas," I said, stepping forward. "The boy is as pure as they come." That was a bit of an exaggeration, but sometimes we embellish when we're trying to make a point. And the point was that my son was not a murderer.

Jasmine was still fiddling with her pockets, trying to pull them out, and her sister turned an exasperated look on her. "What are you doing? We found the murderer."

"I highly doubt that," Mr. Harding said. "He's just a kid."

Jasmine looked between Mr. Harding and her sister, as if unsure what she was supposed to do, but she did stop worrying about the pockets.

Flash lifted his chin in defiance. "I am not. I'm as capable of murder as the rest of you."

I groaned, and Lilly once again clamped her hand over her brother's mouth. Because he routinely entered coding competitions with seasoned men and women, and won, he prided himself on being able to hold his own. But now was not the time for pride.

Amber looked at me, her lips pressed into a tight line. "Your son murdered two people, so what are you going to do about it?"

"You really think this kid killed two grown men?" I asked, gesturing toward Flash, who was struggling under his sister's grip. "The boy hasn't exercised since he was a toddler. And he only exercised then because he had a bad habit of escaping from the house, and I had to chase him."

Flash pulled his sister's hand from his mouth long enough to shout, "Why don't you ever believe I'm just naturally strong and healthy? I don't need exercise. And for the last time, I'm not a kid. I have facial hair and everything."

No, he had two wisps of hair that he occasionally used my tweezers to remove because he was scared of the razor I had bought him for Christmas three years earlier.

Did the boy not realize the kind of trouble he was in? That if he kept talking, he would be restrained and handed over to the police? Because that was the plan if we discovered who was guilty. And because all of us still wore gloves, there wouldn't be any fingerprints on the syringe, just as there was no way to prove who had held the flashlight that had killed Ranger Eric.

The syringe in Flash's pocket was all the proof they needed.

Which gave me pause.

I turned to Benji and lowered my voice. "Two people died, but not in the same manner. The first was with the ranger's flashlight, as if it had been a moment of panic and the killer grabbed the first thing they saw. But the second —they brought that syringe here with a purpose. Whatever liquid was in there, it was premeditated, and they've been carrying it around with them. Why not use the syringe with Eric? More importantly, why not bring two syringes or three or four? Pick a weapon and stick with it."

"You're thinking we're looking for two murderers," Benji said with a thoughtful nod. "The second murderer was waiting for an opportunity. When everyone was standing close to Thomas, it gave them the cover they needed."

I was silent for a moment. How did we even know that Thomas had been the target? Maybe the murderer hadn't cared who they stuck.

"What about Jasmine and Violet?" I asked him, my voice so low, I was unsure if Benji could hear me. "What if the first murder was meant to cover up the second? It didn't matter who died, and it would throw everyone into confusion. In the dark, they could have wildly swung and hit the first person they came in contact with. None of it would make sense, which is exactly what they needed."

Benji hesitated, his nose scrunching up as he thought. "I don't know. I feel like that's a stretch. Those two small women just killed two strong men, and it was premeditated? I mean come on, they're named after flowers."

"Some flowers kill you," I retorted, not liking that he thought women incapable of murder. Or at least, these women. I was just as bad as Flash, trying to prove something that I'd rather not be true.

"That's true, and Jasmine puts you to sleep," he said. "In this case, permanently."

As much as I wanted to, I couldn't discount the sisters as suspects. There weren't many of us left. Outside of my family, there was Jasmine and Violet, Amber, Mr. Harding, and Ranger Charlie.

Speaking of... "Where's Charlie?" I asked, looking around the space. "Was he here when Thomas was...you know..."

"Killed?" Benji asked, his lips quirking up. "It's so cute that regardless of the number of murder investigations you are a part of, you still can't say it."

Cute or not, one of our party was missing.

"Was he?" I repeated.

Benji glanced around the space, as if Ranger Charlie would materialize by our thoughts alone. "I don't know," he admitted. "But if he's our killer, and if he knows more about this maze than he let on, then we're truly stuck down here, with no way to prove he did it."

"Which means the guilt still falls on Flash," I finished.

I spun toward the fractured group, who were all looking at my son like a pack of hyenas who were ready to pounce.

"Before we automatically think a seventeen-year-old boy," I said loudly, "whose only goal in life is to win computer hacking competitions and eat more pizza than should be legally allowed, killed two men tonight, let's first ask the question, 'Where is Ranger Charlie?'"

All heads swiveled at once.

"I swear I saw him just a moment ago," Amber said, spinning in a circle, as if that would help.

Violet looked at me, her eyes troubled. "You think he did it and then made a run for it? That sweet guy? He hardly seems capable."

"And yet my son does?" I retorted, unable to stop my anger from taking over. This was my son they had so callously been talking about.

"Maybe we can all admit that none of us seem like the murdering type, and yet one of us obviously is," Lilly said, just as her brother bit the hand that was still clasped over his mouth. She yelped and let go of him. Not a great start to proving his innocence.

Mr. Harding stepped forward, hands behind his back. "The girl is right, and in my line of business, I've seen it all. Take a bored housewife, for example, who wants more excitement in her life, so she starts dealing drugs out of her basement. In order to cover for all the random cars that show up at the house, she also joins a multilevel marketing company and sells beauty products from her living room. I've also seen a fourteen-year-old computer genius," he gestured to Flash, "who stole five million dollars from a company by hacking into their system. By the time they noticed, the boy had sold his computer to some poor senior citizen who couldn't figure out why the FBI were at her house, as she tried to prove that she didn't even know how to copy and paste text in a document. Eventually they tracked him to a house three streets over."

"Your point?" Amber asked.

Mr. Harding turned a patient smile on her. "That we are all capable of bad things. But also that they were all caught. They thought they had the perfect cover, but it's impossible to remove all evidence. Even if they are wearing gloves." He looked pointedly at all of our gloved hands.

We all were capable of bad things. And even though I knew my family hadn't done it, no one else did. In my mind, we only had five suspects. In their minds, it was nine. Well, eight, not including themselves.

"Which leads us back to Ranger Charlie," Benji said, getting us back on track. "Where is he, and if he's our killer, how are we going to stop him?"

Jasmine spoke from where she'd retreated to one of the far walls. She looked pale, and I wondered how she was still standing. "Let him go. Let him run. If he knows his way out of here, more power to him. If he's the killer, good riddance. That means no one else is going to die. If he's innocent, he'll raise the alarm and get people down here to rescue us."

"The woman has a point," Mr. Harding said. "It feels like a win-win to me."

Amber spun to him. "And where's the justice? Or do journalists not believe in that?"

Mr. Harding only smiled. "We know Charlie's name and what he looks like. How far can he get before the police catch up with him? For right now, I'm more worried about myself. Justice will follow."

Amber didn't look happy about the journalist's answer, but she didn't argue with it either. It made sense.

Until Ranger Charlie walked back into the room, and he was all smiles.

13

"How's everyone holding up?" Ranger Charlie said, walking into the center of the room. "Everyone good?" His smile seemed genuine, and the rest of us looked on in confusion.

"Where have you been?" Violet demanded.

Charlie looked perplexed at her tone of voice. "I stepped around the corner to give myself a pep talk. As the only employee in this group, your safety is my responsibility. That is something that has been grilled into me since day one."

"Isn't today your first day?" Lilly asked.

Charlie held up a finger like he was going to refute her claim but then must have realized she was right because he said slowly, "Technically, yes. But I did attend orientation last week, and Eric brought me through the lower cave two nights ago for additional training. They make certain that we as rangers know our duties to you, the guests of this national park, and our duties to the park itself. We are to take responsibility for both."

Mr. Harding chuckled. "That's great, son. Did you by any chance figure out what to do with the second dead body in that little pep talk of yours?"

Ranger Charlie's complexion immediately emptied of color and now matched the colors of the rocks around us. "Second dead body?"

The journalist had known Charlie hadn't been there and was toying with him. It was mean, but Charlie's reaction only made him laugh harder. "Oh, you weren't here for that? Well, let me fill you in, since it seems you are the safety officer around here. Thomas has been murdered. Which means we now have two dead bodies and the killer is still one of the people in this room. Except this time, he used a syringe, which we found in Flash's pocket. What do you propose we do about that?"

Charlie turned slowly. I knew the exact moment he saw Thomas, laid out on the ground next to Eric, because he immediately ran to a corner and emptied his stomach.

"Can't imagine that's good for the formations we're trying to preserve," Mr. Harding called after him.

I threw a glare at the journalist. "You don't have to be like that. The man has obviously had a shock. No need to play with him like that."

Mr. Harding continued to smile. "I'd hardly call

Charlie a man. He's barely older than your son and doesn't have a clue what he's doing down here."

"But he's trying," I retorted. "And if you don't start being a little nicer, we might just start thinking you are capable of murder. Maybe I'll even be murdered for saying so."

That probably wasn't the wisest thing to say to someone who could be a killer, but at this point, if we didn't want to offend the murderer, we wouldn't be able to talk to anyone.

Now that I thought about it, that wasn't a terrible idea.

"Okay, new plan," I said. "We all find a spot away from each other, we sit, and we wait. No talking. No moving. That way, no one can get close enough to anyone else for there to be another...incident."

Jasmine nodded in agreement and immediately plunked herself down. "I found my spot."

The others gave resigned sighs, and each set about finding their waiting place.

"I wish I at least had a video game," Flash said. "But someone wouldn't let me put it in her backpack." He threw an accusatory look in my direction. As if it was my fault we were stuck down in the caverns with no guide and a murderer on the loose. As if I should have predicted that we'd be sitting for several hours on cold rocks, waiting to be rescued.

"And when you have a full battery later when we're driving back, you'll thank me," I said, sending him a smile in return. It was a strained smile, but it was better than nothing and was all I could muster at the moment.

And then we sat. Silent. For what felt like hours.

In reality, it was twenty minutes before someone couldn't take it anymore and spoke.

"This is dumb," Amber said, standing up. "What if they never realize we're gone? Are we really just going to wait down here until we starve to death? They won't even realize that two of us were murdered, because it will be a dozen bodies they find."

Amber was obviously a doer. Someone who couldn't stand to wait for things to happen. I understood her sentiment. When I'd lived in the big city, if I'd had to make a doctor's appointment, I would have rather driven twenty minutes to a farther location than visit an office that was just down the street but required I wait twenty minutes in traffic.

"What would you rather do?" Violet asked in a tired voice. "We're cold. Hungry. And have no idea where we are. If we try to find our way back, we could end up more lost, and then no one would ever find us."

Amber stuck her hands on her hips. "I'd rather actually do something to protect ourselves. I suggest we use something to create makeshift handcuffs for the boy, since he's the one who had the syringe. Right now the assumption is that he's the killer. We then form a train, checking each possible route, and leave markers with bits of stalactites everywhere we go, so that even if we do get lost, our potential rescuers will be able to follow the trail."

"By the boy, I'm assuming you mean my son," I said, standing. "And we're not doing that. That will make him an easy target for whoever the real killer is. Maybe that's your intention."

Amber laughed, though it was devoid of humor. "You think I'm the murderer. That I killed my boyfriend."

"Please. You didn't even like the guy. Your body language said it all," I said, taking a step toward her. "You avoided him unless it was advantageous for you to do otherwise. And he knew it. That was why he broke up with you. You know, right before he died."

Amber glared at me. I knew it was risky, allowing myself to get her riled up like this, but the tension was too heavy and too thick. I was tired, and I just wanted all this to be over. People made mistakes when they were angry. Said things they didn't mean to say. And if I could get enough people angry, someone was sure to spill something they shouldn't.

Or someone else would end up dead.

The available options weren't great.

"If you're so smart, why would I kill Eric, when it was Thomas I was annoyed with?" Amber asked.

I shrugged. "I don't know. You're the killer. You tell me."

Amber let out a sarcastic "Ha!" And then she burst into tears.

That hadn't been what I'd expected.

"You don't know what it's like to see someone wither before your very eyes," she said through her sobs. She wasn't even looking at me anymore, her face buried in her hands. "To see someone so full of life realize he's been taken advantage of, that someone he thought was his friend has turned on him. That he was nothing to anyone except a puppet. He was too trusting and thought of everyone as inherently good. And they knew it." She sniffed and wiped at her eyes. "It broke him. These last few months, he'd given up and accepted his fate—someone who wasn't capable of living his own life, always at the whims of others. I tried getting him to walk away. He said he couldn't. He was in too deep. And now look at him." Amber glanced over at Thomas and burst into another round of tears.

And now I felt horrible. I had caused this. This was what I got for pushing people's buttons. I never would have done this type of thing in a therapy session. And this was why.

"I'm so sorry," I said, backing up but with nowhere to hide.

Violet was watching me with a thoughtful expression. "Anyone think the psychologist talks too much?" she asked slowly. "She's always taking charge and coming up with the plan. She and her family were the ones who first examined Eric's body. She was having a therapy session with Thomas mere minutes before he collapsed. And the syringe was found on her son."

Mr. Harding's smug expression morphed into contemplation. "I think you're on to something. And we've all had a terrible time figuring out who it was, because it wasn't any one person. It was a family affair. The boy already admitted they know their way around a murder scene."

Amber hesitated, not looking like she was convinced, but everyone else was looking at us like we were lunch.

Charlie stepped in front of me and held out his hands. I'd never thought it would be him who might save us—he didn't exactly have the most commanding presence—but at that moment, he was the only thing keeping the others at bay.

"Now hold on," he said. "Murderers or not, I'm bound by my oath to keep everyone on this tour safe. Everyone. That includes the Swallows family."

Well, it wasn't exactly a vote of confidence in our favor, but it was something, and I'd take it.

"Besides," he continued, "I have a better idea."

14

Ranger Charlie reached into his backpack and pulled something out. I craned my neck, but I couldn't see what it was. Handcuffs, maybe. Something to detain us, as everyone was so determined to do. Maybe he wouldn't allow harm to come to us, but that didn't mean he was going to make life comfortable. And all the while, a murderer would be walking around, inwardly congratulating themselves on a job well done.

But when Charlie turned around, he wasn't holding handcuffs. He was holding beef jerky in one hand and what looked like a card game in the other.

"We're all getting cranky," he said with his signature goofy smile. "We've been down here for a couple of hours now. We're cold and tired and hungry. That can cause us to see things differently than they really are. The Swallows family doesn't seem to be an immediate threat to anyone, so before we do something rash, I propose we share my beef jerky and play a round of Uno."

Beef jerky did sound really good.

"Hang on," Violet said, holding up a finger. "We weren't supposed to bring food on this tour. The instructions were very specific."

A look of guilt passed over Charlie's expression, and his smile turned shy. "That's true." He waved the large package at us. "But it's beef jerky, so no crumbs. And I certainly wouldn't do something like litter down here."

"I'm not going to complain," Flash said, stepping toward the jerky. Everyone else flinched, like he was about to go into another murderous rage. He stopped and looked back at me with confusion. "I'm really hungry, guys. I didn't kill anyone, but if I don't get some food in me, that may become a very real possibility."

And now my son was threatening that if he didn't eat Charlie's snacks, he'd literally kill someone. Awesome.

"What he means," I said, stepping forward, "is that Charlie is right. We all need to get our blood sugar up a little, and a card game would be a great way to cut the tension."

Charlie sent me a look of gratitude and then turned back to everyone. "Because we have so many people, let's start with two pieces of jerky each. I know it's not much, but at least we'll get a little protein in us." He moved around the group, offering food, as if they wouldn't dare hurt him. And it left me wondering if he was smarter than he let on. In a situation like this, you don't hurt the one who is contributing to the group. Charlie was sharing food and offering entertainment. The person they would most likely turn on was the one who didn't have anything to offer. I had given therapy sessions, but because Thomas had died almost immediately after returning to the group, that made my contribution null and void.

And right now, Flash was showing he was the type of person who tended to take resources from the group. If food was available, he'd eat the entire thing without a thought for others who might not have eaten. His stomach controlled his thoughts and behavior, and people were starting to see that.

Right now, he was the weak link.

What was something we could contribute to the group —something that would show we were the good guys? How could we prove that we wanted what was best for everyone, and that that didn't include killing them off, one by one?

Anything therapy related was out of the question, and yet there were some people we knew nothing about. The journalist, for one. Mr. Harding was the biggest question mark here.

"We probably have a couple hours before people notice we're missing," I said. "Uno seems like a fun game but requires us to be in close proximity to each other, and I don't feel comfortable with us splitting off in smaller groups." There we go. Let them know I don't want to isolate people like the murderer would want. "What if we played a group game where we don't have to sit right next to each other? Earlier someone mentioned the game two truths and a lie."

"That was me," Violet said. "But it's a game that is best for the sneaky and manipulative type, because they want to create an image of themselves without anyone realizing they're doing it. Best case scenario, you're playing with honest people who want to use it as an excuse to brag without coming across as conceited. Worst case scenario, you're playing with a bunch of liars who want to portray themselves as something they're not." She paused, her gaze boring into me. "Is that the game you'd like to play?"

I guess not.

"No, just curious if anyone had played it. Maybe you have a game you'd like to recommend. Something to pass the time."

Violet was looking at me like she didn't trust me, which I realized was fair under the circumstances. No one should trust anyone. Not with two people dead. I certainly didn't trust her, or anyone else here outside my family. Though, for some reason, I trusted Charlie. I couldn't help but like him.

Maybe that was a problem.

"I don't play games," she finally said.

"Not everyone does," I said. "Nothing wrong with that. But I really don't want to sit here staring at each other for the next two or three hours."

She watched me another minute longer. "Let's have a mock trial, then. Let's pass the time by finding our killer so I don't end up next."

"That seems like something best left to the authorities." I didn't allow my gaze to waver. "What would we do with the person, or people, once we come to a verdict?"

Violet hesitated, as if she thought this was a trick of some kind. But I was honestly curious. It wasn't that I didn't want to know who the murderer was—I desperately did. But right now, all the evidence pointed to my family, and I didn't think a trial by our peers would go very well. There were four of us and five of them, if Charlie decided to take their side.

It could only end badly.

"We'd tie them up, I suppose," Violet said. That seemed fair. "And then we'd leave them in a far corner where no one would think to look while the rest of us were rescued. If questions were asked, we'd tell the authorities that you were supposed to be on this tour but you were a no-show."

That was not so fair. And from the sounds of it, she had already determined my family were the killers and she'd have no problem leaving us there to rot.

"But what if we were wrong?" I asked. "What if we made a mistake, the real murderer was led to freedom, and innocent people died because of what we did? Do you really want something like that on your conscience? Because I assure you, if you are as good a person as you want us to believe, it would haunt you for the rest of your life."

That quieted Violet. She opened her mouth to speak, but no words came out for a moment. "That is a point I hadn't considered."

"It had crossed my mind," Mr. Harding said. "And it likely occurred to anyone else whose intentions are pure."

Violet paled, as if just now realizing that her aggressive need to find the killer had actually placed her in the crosshairs. "You can't honestly believe I killed those two men. I'd never met either of them. Why aren't you looking at the boy who literally had the murder weapon in his pocket?"

"Once again, not a boy," Flash said, throwing his arms in the air and releasing an exasperated sigh.

I ignored him.

"But you did know of one of them," I said. "Your sister had an online relationship with a man who broke her heart. That's why you were here. To confront him. You don't think that's motive? I've met sisters who would kill for their family."

"I'm not one of them," Violet said, now looking panicked. "And neither is Jasmine. Yes, she wanted to confront him in person. He's always come up with an excuse why he couldn't meet her. Two years of that. That's why it was so important that he look her in the eyes and finally face what he did. But we wouldn't have killed him over that."

I glanced at Jasmine and immediately regretted my decision to call Violet out. I shouldn't have said anything—those things had been told in confidence. Yes, the therapy office may have been a bit unorthodox, but I was still bound to protect the privacy of my patients. It had been a moment of panic—a moment where I had been trying to throw suspicion on anyone but myself and my family. An act of self-preservation.

And it had been wrong.

"I'm so sorry," I said. "I didn't mean to—"

"Of course you meant to," Jasmine spat out. "Up until this moment, I didn't agree with my sister. There was no way you could harm someone. Not after what we talked through. I trusted you." She slapped away the tears that had sprung to her eyes. "But now I realize I was taken for a fool. I believe you killed those two men. And maybe your family didn't help, but they allowed it. Dr. Swallows, you're as guilty as they come. And I don't care what kind of justice comes your way, as long as you suffer."

Well, that could have gone better.

The five in our group who weren't a part of the Swallows clan now stood huddled on the opposite side of the cavern, presumably trying to figure out what to do with us. From all the anxious looks that were being thrown our way, it couldn't be anything good. No one was on our side now. Not even Charlie.

"I'm sorry," I told Benji and the kids. "This is all my fault. I misused my position as a confidante, caring more about finding clues than helping people. And now we're all going to pay for it."

"This isn't your fault," Benji said. "They're acting out of fear. Two people are dead, and all signs point to us. Yes, Violet and Jasmine had a connection to either Eric or Thomas, but that's not enough right now."

"It's not like I had motive," I said, crossing my arms

over my chest. It was starting to feel colder down here. Or maybe that was the chill of my impending doom. "I hadn't met the two men before coming here. Isn't that more important than circumstantial evidence?"

"What we need is to find real evidence," Lilly said. "You said you were looking for clues. What have you found so far?"

That was a good question. And a depressing one. "Nothing," I said. "I honestly don't have a single clue. Anything Thomas might have told me doesn't matter, because he's dead. I can tell Violet has a lot of repressed anger, but that doesn't make her a killer. Most of the country has repressed anger of some sort. Mr. Harding I could see killing someone. He's an obnoxious journalist who came here to do a piece on the Carlsbad Caverns and now has a front row seat to a murder mystery. Journalists are known for doing anything to get a story, but would he really stoop to taking people's lives?"

"We have five suspects and, aside from Charlie, they all have motive to kill one of the men, but not both," Flash said slowly. "Except Mr. Harding. The more people who die, the bigger the story, right?"

He had a point. But I wasn't convinced it was Mr. Harding. He was too...obvious.

"Dad always said serial killers have one method they use," Lilly said. "Ed Gein, Ted Bundy, H.H. Holmes—they all had a specific way they did things. It wasn't like they were out there on the streets, killing whoever they saw with anything they could get their hands on."

I didn't miss those family dinner conversations. Somehow Cameron had always managed to bring the topic back to his area of expertise, the psychology of serial killers. I'd always hated it, but Lilly had a point. And thinking like killers could prove useful right now. Because my expertise, the psychology of normal people, wasn't working out so well.

"But we have two very different methods here," Flash said. "One victim was bludgeoned. That seems more personal and done out of anger. Rage. Thomas was given something in a syringe, which has a very different feel to it. That's more like someone had a job to do. Maybe someone here is a nurse or doctor. They are also more likely to be a woman."

Lilly held up a finger. "Or a man who is methodical. Someone who doesn't like to deal with mess."

I shared a sad look with Benji. This was supposed to be a family vacation to relax, have fun, and spend time together before the kids moved away. This was not the vacation I had wanted.

"The syringe doesn't tell us anything about the person," I said, sighing. "Yes, they are methodical. And yes, they had a job to do. They came prepared. But they used a syringe so they could frame someone else. It was small and easy to slip into someone's pocket."

Flash's lips parted. "That's diabolical."

"Yes, it is."

"So, are we looking for one person, or are we looking for two?" Lilly asked.

I watched as the others deliberated our fate. Did I really think the two sisters capable of something like this?

Violet turned to us, cutting off any answer I may have had, which was just as well. Because I didn't know the answer.

"It's been decided," she said. The others avoided looking at us, which gave me a pretty good clue to what that decision had been. They were going to tie us up and leave us in a dark corner somewhere.

"Look, I'm going to save you the trouble," Flash said, then he turned and ran at full speed in the direction we'd entered the cavern from.

I looked on in horror. "What does he think he's doing? He won't find the ladders we came down. Not with all the twists and turns and side tunnels. He has a terrible sense of direction. The boy got lost walking to school every day, and we only live a few blocks away."

Violet turned slowly toward me, blinking rapidly, like she was unsure what had just happened. I knew the feeling well.

"We were just going to take your headlamps so you couldn't escape," she said.

I looked up at the ceiling. If any one of those stalactites fell on me and I didn't have a helmet, I'd be a goner. "Yeah,

I don't think so. I'm not wishing for a death by stalactite. There have to be better ways to go."

Violet looked at the others. "We'd come to the conclusion that you wouldn't attempt to frame your own son, so he likely acted alone and you were trying to cover for him. His running confirms our suspicions." She glanced nervously in the direction he'd disappeared. "But I don't want to go after him."

Mr. Harding frowned. "No one is going after him. He's on his own now."

And now I had a dilemma. Go after Flash and risk not finding him and getting lost myself, as well as leaving Benji and Lilly alone with a serial killer.

Or stay and hope Flash would miraculously find his way out.

I didn't like either option.

Neither did Amber, apparently.

"You people are insane," she muttered, nervously pulling on her ponytail.

Mr. Harding leaned in closer, mocking her as he pulled on his ear. "What was that?"

"You're insane," Amber said louder. "Don't you see what's happening? It's turning all *Lord of the Flies*. We're trapped in a place together and going feral, turning on one another."

"Yeah, because two people are dead. Including your boyfriend," Violet said. "It's us against them. There's no way around that."

Chaos. That was what this was. And you couldn't reason with people when they were in this state of mind.

I thought back to the conversation my family had been having before Flash took off. He and Lilly had been talking about the person who had killed Thomas being methodical. Calculated.

And that was when I saw it for what it was. Calculated chaos.

"This is what the murderer wants," I said. The others stopped talking and looked at me, seeming annoyed that I dared interrupt their argument with something that might resemble rationality. "Think about it. You just said there is no way around us dividing ourselves into us versus them. Thinking like that only benefits the killer, because then no one is looking at him, or her. Right now, we're looking at everyone as two groups. Not individuals."

I once again looked in the direction Flash had escaped, knowing what I had to do. "I'm going after my son, because I'm not going to let you people be the reason he ends up injured, or worse. In the meantime, please attempt to not play into the murderer's hands. They have the advantage here. And spoiler alert, it's not Flash."

And then I walked away, my head held high, because I couldn't let them see anything but confidence coming from me. I had no idea if they would listen, but right now, that was the least of my concerns.

When I reached the edge of the cavern room, I hesitated. The path narrowed here.

"Flash," I called. "Come on back. They're not going to do anything to you."

No answer.

It was dark up ahead, especially with only the one headlamp. When it had been all of us, we'd had enough light that I'd never felt nervous. Now, shadows surrounded me, and I could see how easy it would be to get turned around.

I took a step forward, fairly certain nothing lived in these caverns. Even if there were bats hanging around, they wouldn't want anything to do with me and my head-lamp. I took a few more steps forward, realizing there were actually plenty of directions I could go in from here, but it was difficult to see them all with only my one source of light. I had to stop every few steps and swing my head around to understand exactly what my options were.

"Flash, you need to come back," I tried again. My voice shook, from both the cold and fear. What if Flash had gotten himself completely lost, running in whichever direction pleased him, and he wasn't able to find his way back? Or more frightening, what if we weren't able to find him either?

I didn't want to go too far, not wanting to place myself in a similar situation, and I found myself conflicted on what to do.

And then a hand landed on my shoulder.

"Leaving the group was a mistake," a man's voice said.

I screamed.

16

Mr. Harding.

I had to lower my gaze to avoid being blinded by his headlamp.

"Sorry to startle you," he said. "But you need to come back now."

I shook my head, willing my heart to calm. "Thank you for your concern, but I have to find my son. I know you all think he's a murderer, but he's not. He's the sweetest guy around, and he has no reason to kill anyone. Especially two random people he literally just met. And how would he have arranged to be on this tour? I was the one who planned the vacation and bought tickets and—"

Mr. Harding held up a hand, stopping my rambling mid-sentence. "I know. And we'll find him. But that's not what I meant when I said it was a mistake to leave."

I studied Mr. Harding, and my heart picked up speed. "You're right. I shouldn't have left." I stepped around the journalist to return the way I had come. "It felt wrong not to follow Flash, though."

Mr. Harding didn't follow me. "It was a mistake to leave, because you were right about the murderer. You saw with your own eyes, the two men didn't have to wander away from the cavern for the murderer to strike. In fact, this group is what has hidden them. It's what has made each of us a suspect. Everyone was there. Both times. No one is safe."

"So, theoretically, I should be safer here, then. Away from the group," I said, glancing over my shoulder.

"Theoretically, yes," Mr. Harding said. "Unless the murderer followed you."

My heart pounded in my ears, and the room started to spin. I squeezed my eyes shut, forcing my breaths to slow. I turned toward the cavern and quickened my steps, trying to keep my focus off Mr. Harding, who was keeping pace with me.

"Why?" I couldn't think of anything else to ask. Not when my kids were about to lose their mother. "Why kill those people? Why kill me? To what end?"

Silence.

"Because you have made yourself an easy target." A pause. "But two victims in the past two hours is plenty. We don't need a third. And certainly not someone as intelligent and accomplished as yourself."

So, Mr. Harding didn't have any intention of killing me. Or he was just trying to get me to trust him so I wouldn't suspect him of the first two deaths.

"What do you know about me and my accomplishments?" I asked, my steps slowing. I turned around. If he was going to take me out, it wasn't going to be in the dark or through an injection. He was going to have to look me in the eyes.

The journalist smiled. He might have meant it to be reassuring, but I only saw it as threatening. Something he might do to lure someone into a false sense of security.

"I knew I recognized your last name, Swallows, though I was having trouble remembering from where," he said. "You were married to Dr. Cameron Swallows. I did a piece on him a few years ago in preparation for his first book's debut. It's a fascinating read—he has a really interesting take on serial killers."

"We divorced a few years ago," I said, tense. I did find it ironic that my family was in this situation, when we knew so much about how serial killers worked, thanks to my ex-husband's love of bringing work home, and yet, that knowledge hadn't helped us in the slightest.

Mr. Harding raised his hands as if to say, *what can you do?*

I stayed silent, studying him. If Mr. Harding was the killer, then this was a game for him. He'd laid out a puzzle, and he wanted to know if I would be able to piece it together. There was a thrill, wondering if he would be caught or if he truly was smarter than everyone around him.

"You must have a take on what's happening here," he finally said. "Your ex-husband is the best in his field."

I puffed out my chest and looked Mr. Harding straight in the eye. "What I know is that the only reason I'm standing here in this corridor of rock is because of my family. They are the reason I do everything. That includes catching a killer, if it comes down to it. And believe me when I say, we are going to walk out of this place alive." I spun back toward where I thought the cavern was. I shouldn't have allowed Mr. Harding to distract me from my surroundings. I glanced over my shoulder. "And yes, that was a threat."

And then I walked off, not daring to look back.

"Mom!"

Flash ran at me as soon as I stepped into the main cavern. He practically knocked me over as he crushed me in a bear hug. "We've been so worried."

I pulled back, balking. "*You've* been worried? I left because you charged out of here like you had a death wish. How did you even make it back?"

He grinned. "I only left the room as a dramatic exit so I could get the focus off you. Then I used the strategy I do with corn mazes—I just kept making a right turn every chance I got until I eventually ended up back here, but on the opposite side of the cavern."

I couldn't believe that had worked, and I wouldn't have risked my life like he had. But I was grateful to Flash, regardless. I had raised a good kid. And if the others couldn't see it, that was on them.

"How has everyone been treating you?" I asked, my voice low. "They give you any trouble?"

Flash hesitated, which meant yes but he didn't want me to worry. "All I know is that we need to solve this thing."

That was when I saw the fear in his eyes. He was still all smiles, but that was for my benefit. Flash was scared. I'd never known my son to be afraid of anything, always jumping in head first and asking questions later.

This was uncharted territory, and my heart immediately constricted.

Lilly tackled me before I could respond, followed by Benji.

"That is the last time anyone leaves this room alone," he said, placing one hand on each of my cheeks and pulling me in for a kiss.

For once, the kids didn't protest at the open display of affection. As much as they loved Benji, they had no desire to watch me kissing him.

I pulled back and ruffled Benji's hair. "It will be difficult to hold a family meeting in this kind of situation." I threw a glance at Flash. "Just after you left, I gave a speech about how the murderer wants to get lost in the crowd and we should be looking at each other as individuals rather than us versus them. If we want to get out of this thing unscathed, any discussion we have needs to be an open conversation between all members of the group. No one escapes scrutiny, including us. We have to show we have nothing to hide."

Benji's lips pressed into a tight line. "That's a risky move."

I gave a single nod. "I know." And then I wrapped my arms around his waist and held on for dear life. He returned the hug, and we just stood there for what felt like forever. In that moment, I needed to hold on to one of the few people left in my life who was strong and stable. Someone I could count on. And he was the warmth I needed, both literally and figuratively.

When Flash cleared his throat, reminding me of his presence, I pulled back. I immediately missed Benji's warmth, but we had two murders to solve.

"I know it's risky," I said. "But I don't see any way around it. We have nothing to hide, so we have nothing to fear."

"Yeah, except someone here isn't above planting evidence," Flash said.

That was a good point, and one I had already considered.

"You're right. But repeatedly telling people that you're innocent isn't convincing anyone. We need to raise doubt, shine the light on other possibilities. Preferably ones that don't include the four of us."

Benji released a long sigh and rubbed his eyebrows. "Your mom is right, of course. We can't do this on our own, and if we try, it's only going to make things worse. We need to get someone else to advocate for us."

Mr. Harding.

The name popped into my head, and I immediately dismissed it. He was the best candidate to be our murderer. The man was fascinated by serial killers and had read into their psychology. He knew who I was. Who my ex-husband was. He appeared to be a loner, and as a journalist, he would benefit professionally as a witness to a double homicide.

But just in case he wasn't the murderer, he was also the best candidate to be our advocate.

He wasn't emotional like the others, and when he spoke, people tended to listen.

"Benji, I think it should be you who calls the meeting," I said, turning to him. "I think they're tired of hearing from me, if Violet's accusations are anything to go by."

Benji slipped his hand into mine and squeezed it. "If you're sure."

Was I?

Nope. But by my estimation, we had another thirty

minutes until the tour was supposed to conclude, and another two or three hours until anyone on the outside noticed we'd gone missing. Unless we got lucky and Charlie or Eric was supposed to lead another tour this afternoon.

"I'm sure," I said. "We can't risk the alternative."

17

"I want to thank you all for agreeing to this conversation," Benji said, looking around at the others, who had gathered in a circle. We were all standing because we were too cold to sit on the rocks anymore. It was probably for the best, because I didn't want to do any more damage than we'd already likely done. We'd all leaned against or sat on the formations as we attempted to make our imprisonment more comfortable throughout the previous couple of hours. Something we definitely weren't supposed to do.

"It's not like we had a choice to be here," Amber said. "Where were we going to go?"

Violet chimed in, looking straight at me. "But if you think this is going to get your son off the hook, you're sorely mistaken. Did he come back? Yes. But I would have too, if my only alternative was dying alone in an isolated underground chamber."

I folded my arms and nodded, mostly because I was freezing and I didn't want them to mistake my shaking for fear.

"I get it. The syringe was found in his pocket. It's a little too convenient if you ask me, but still, it's the only thing you have to go on."

Flash threw me an accusatory glare, and I gave him what I hoped he'd interpret as an apologetic smile. I had to admit, though, that if I were in their shoes, I would absolutely be taking a closer look at him. Their lives were on the line.

Mr. Harding grunted. "He didn't actually do it, though. I mean, look at the boy. I doubt he's ever stepped foot outside. He's practically albino."

"Why does everyone insist on picking on me?" he protested. "I do get outside, and I am capable of all sorts of things." He paused and looked at the ceiling, as if he were trying to come up with an example. "Like last week," he finally said. "I went on a walk while carrying weights."

I supposed his walk could be redefined as that. He'd carried his computer to the local electronics shop so it could be serviced, before he'd hurried home so he could code on his backup computer. His computers were in constant rotation considering how much time he spent on them.

Mr. Harding raised an eyebrow and gestured to Flash. "See what I mean?"

"I've read articles," Jasmine said. "These boys play violent video games, and then it instills a need to reenact it in real life. All that shooting and harming virtual people isn't healthy for this generation's young people."

"You aren't much older than him," Lilly said, standing up for her brother. "You're what, twenty or something?"

Jasmine beamed. "Twenty-six, but thank you. I have been told I look young for my age."

Oh, that was smart. Lilly had been trying to get Jasmine as an ally by subtly complimenting her, and judging by Jasmine's large smile, it may have worked.

"The point is," I said, "there is a murderer among us. And we need to have a discussion, shining a light on each person in this circle, until we know who it is. I agree with you that that person cannot be allowed to walk out of here as a free person. And yes, Flash may have had the syringe. But he lacks motive. Why would an otherwise healthy, happy, successful teenage boy decide to go on a murderous rampage and kill two people? It doesn't make sense."

"She has a point," Mr. Harding said.

I turned to him, my eyebrows dipping.

"What?" he asked when I didn't say anything.

"You keep agreeing with me," I said slowly. "And don't get me wrong, I'm grateful. But I also find it suspicious."

"Would you rather have me make a case against the boy?" he asked, his lips pulling up into a slight smile. "I can do that if you like. I can make a case against everyone in this room."

That gave me pause. Mr. Harding was a journalist, but he'd never met us until today. He shouldn't know anything about anyone, other than what he'd observed. And as a psychologist, I prided myself on picking out the finer details people didn't realize they were putting on display. What could he possibly know that I didn't?

"All right," I said. "Have at it."

"If we all turned our headlamps off," Flash whispered to Lilly, "this would be a real-life version of the game Murder in the Dark. You know, how everyone tries to convince everyone else they didn't do it and who the real murderer is. And the murder always happens in the dark, hence the name."

Unfortunately, Flash's whisper was more akin to a hoarse half-shout, so everyone heard.

"You're enjoying this?" Amber asked. Her voice held a warning that I hoped Flash would understand.

He seemed confused on what the correct answer to this question was, so she continued. "My boyfriend is dead. Our guide is dead. We are stuck a thousand feet underground. And in my estimation, a serial killer is the only person who would see that as a game."

"I misspoke," Flash said slowly. I released a sigh of relief. "I meant an adventure. You know, like one of those escape rooms."

I wanted to smack my palm against my forehead, but I

tried not to react to my son's impulsivity. It was what made Flash the hilarious, sweet, wonderful person he was. But his cluelessness had also gotten him into trouble more times than I could count, and not everyone appreciated his...uniqueness.

"Amber, you say your boyfriend is dead like it's a bad thing," I interrupted before Flash could bury himself in a hole deeper than he already had.

It was my turn to be on the receiving end of her glare, but that is what moms do. They take one for the team, and if we were going to examine each person individually, might as well start with her.

"What are you saying?" she asked.

I raised a shoulder, like I hadn't had anything in mind. "Just that I noticed you avoided physical contact with Thomas from the moment you two entered the orientation room till the moment he died."

"And even then, your performance wasn't convincing," Mr. Harding added. It turned out we could count on him as an ally. For now. And I'd take it as long as he was willing to keep the heat off my family. "I mean, all that tearless wailing when he dropped in front of us. It was almost as if you had expected it."

Amber's gaze hardened. "Did Thomas and I have our share of problems? Yes. But I didn't kill him."

"What kind of problems?" Mr. Harding pushed. I didn't think Amber would answer him, especially not in front of everyone like this, but then her shoulders slumped.

"He was constantly working late. If he received a text or a call from the jewelry store, he'd drop everything and rush over there. They owned his soul. He was also quite gullible, always believing everything he was told. It didn't matter if it was a rich sheik from the Middle East who wanted to bestow his wealth or a grandma who sent him an email claiming to have lost her life savings, he was always sending money somewhere. How could I marry someone who would singlehandedly send us into bankruptcy?"

"And you'd had a fight about that just before coming to the caverns?" I asked, taking over.

She nodded. "A guy at work had recommended the caverns, but I wanted to go somewhere with a beach. Thomas seemed to listen to everyone other than me, though."

"I can only imagine how angry you were with him once you realized we were trapped down here," Mr. Harding said. "I mean, it was his fault you two were down here in the first place."

Amber's bottom lip trembled. "I was angry, yes. But I would never kill that infuriating goofball. Even if I couldn't marry him, I did love him."

Not only that, it wouldn't explain Ranger Eric's death. Amber could have killed Thomas, but she'd have no reason to kill the ranger. She hadn't wanted to be down here in the first place.

"The purpose of our being gathered," I said, "is to

discover who the murderer is. It could be one person—a serial killer. But it can also be two different people. I propose we consider Amber as innocent of Eric's death but a viable suspect in Thomas's. Do I have anyone who would like to second that motion?"

Everyone looked at me like I was crazy, treating this like a business meeting. But I didn't know how else to do it. Throwing out accusations and causing panic wasn't helping, and if we took emotion out of it, we were more likely to act with our heads rather than impulsively through our hearts. Having Flash as a son, I knew all about where impulsivity could get you.

"I want to go on record that I think this is weird," Violet said. "But I'll second your motion."

I gave her a smile. "If we had someone recording minutes, they would write down your opinion that this is weird. And for the same record, I agree with you."

Mr. Harding was giving me an annoyed look, maybe because he was used to being the one asking questions, and maybe I was stepping on his toes. But it was dangerous to have a single person in charge of everything at this point, even he had to agree with that. But as a sort of peace offering, I asked, "Who do you think we should consider next, Mr. Harding?"

He considered me for a moment, maybe trying to figure out if this was a trap, before turning to Benji. "Let's look at your boyfriend, shall we?"

I swallowed hard, trying to remind myself that I had

nothing to worry about. Benji had no connection to either of those men.

Benji didn't allow it to visibly ruffle him. Instead, he smiled and said, "Fiancé. We're getting married in three weeks."

"Congratulations," Mr. Harding said, though not sounding like he cared either way. "Let's talk about you being the strongest one in this cavern. Killing a man with a flashlight? Easy peasy. From what I understand, you're no stranger to murder in your little town. Murders seem to follow Maddie and her family everywhere she goes. And being engaged to her, I'd bet you'd do anything for her."

18

Mr. Harding was no ally. He was a piranha. And he was out for blood. How did he even know anything about my town, or my family? Sure, he had done a piece on Cameron and his research on the psychology of serial killers, but my ex-husband had never lived in Amor in his life, and we'd had limited contact since the divorce. There was no reason Mr. Harding should know anything beyond what his story required.

"I help the police sometimes," I said. "As a professional. My skills as a psychologist are useful in investigations. Benji didn't know Ranger Eric or Thomas. He has no motive. And someone shouldn't be accused of murder just because they have muscles. He's a handyman. It comes with the territory."

Benji discreetly squeezed my arm. It seemed to be

intended both for reassurance and as a warning. "It will be better if I speak for myself," he murmured.

My face flushed with embarrassment. I was meddling, like I always did, never trusting others to be able to take care of themselves. I had gotten that lovely attribute from my mother, and at times, it seemed impossible to keep it at bay.

"I sense an accusation in there," Benji said to Mr. Harding, offering him an amused smile. How did he always manage to be so calm? He should be freaking out right now. At least then I would feel somewhat normal in my reaction. Thank goodness he wasn't me.

"Yes, there is," Mr. Harding said. "I'm not sure how, but these murders are connected to the Swallows family, and because of your connection to Maddie, you have, unfortunately, been lumped in with them. Even if you're just covering for Maddie, that still makes you an accomplice."

Benji fixed a thoughtful stare on the journalist. "What makes you so sure it's this family, when we have no connection to either of the victims? You have a woman who tracked down a man who cheated on her." He nodded to Jasmine. "And a woman who was in an unhappy relationship with Thomas." He gestured toward Amber. "An overprotective sister." His gaze landed on Violet before returning to Mr. Harding. "And yet your sights have landed on us."

Mr. Harding held Benji's gaze, as if they were in a staring contest and he didn't want to lose. "After I wrote my piece on Cameron Swallows and his research, I became increasingly fascinated with this man, as well as his family. I did know of his divorce, and that his wife and children had moved to a small New Mexican town. I couldn't help but assume that Cameron was more macabre than he let on in the interview, that it was the reason behind the divorce, and I was determined to speak with her."

I shared a confused look with Benji. "That was years ago, and I never heard from you. Didn't receive any phone calls or emails."

Mr. Harding nodded. "No, I was given other assignments that took precedence over a divorcee. But then imagine my surprise when I heard of a double murder in that small town you'd moved to. A coincidence, I was sure. And yet, more news stories came up. Other small New Mexican towns that didn't have much going on and where murder is kind of a big deal. Your name kept appearing." He paused for dramatic effect. "A new question presented itself. Maybe it wasn't you who'd left Cameron but the other way around. Maybe he knew who you really were. A murderer. An expert at reading people—and framing them."

I narrowed my eyes. "And you think he'd allow me to leave with the children if that were the case?"

Mr. Harding shrugged. "I'm just telling you what I've noticed. Imagine my shock this morning to find we were on this tour together. Of course, I wasn't as surprised as the rest of you when two men died. Why would I be? You're here."

I stared, unsure how to respond to his allegations. Mr. Harding was right. Murder did seem to follow me around, but it wasn't intentional. And I remained surprised every time it happened.

A small light distracted me from my thoughts, and I glanced at his pocket. "You're recording again, aren't you? And not for your piece on the Carlsbad Caverns."

A smile crept over his face. "Oh, there is certainly going to be a story on the Carlsbad Caverns, but it is no longer the formations that will take center stage. You've given me something far better, Maddie Swallows."

I released a defeated sigh. "Is that why you followed me when I left to find Flash? Were you hoping to corner me into a confession, or at least an interview?"

"Something like that."

Ranger Charlie was looking at me with shock and disappointment. "I trusted you," he said, his voice breaking. "You said you wanted to keep people safe."

I couldn't stand the way he was looking at me—like I had betrayed him.

"I swear I had nothing to do with any of those murders," I told him, my eyes pleading with him to believe me. "Yes, it's true, they seem to happen more often than is normal whenever I'm around. But it's more like I'm in the wrong place at the right time. Once was a coincidence, twice was ridiculous. Now? I don't know what to think.

Maybe God, or the universe, or whatever you believe in, sends me to these places on purpose. Like it knows I can help. I have gifts that can bring justice in a world where criminals escape punishment."

"That is what law enforcement is for," Mr. Harding chided, clicking his tongue in disapproval. "And I don't believe the universe has appointed you as a vigilante. If that were the case, wouldn't it be better to stop the murders from happening before they occurred?"

I threw my arms into the air. "I don't know, okay? All I'm saying is that my purpose in life is to help, not harm. I hated the family dinners when Cameron would bring up his research. It hurt even hearing about the things he thought about each day. It changed him. It changed our relationship. And I had to leave." My voice had risen, and I hated myself for sharing so much with people who didn't care. Who only wanted to see us convicted for something we hadn't done. They didn't deserve an explanation, not when there were others who had actual motives.

Leave it to me to get us on a tour with the one person in the whole place who knew who I was and what my family had gone through. The one person who wanted to use us as a spectacle and turn our lives into a story people could gossip about.

"I'm not going to let you do this to my family," I said, my voice quieting. "They don't deserve to be splashed across the internet, like they've done something wrong for just existing."

Mr. Harding's lips were pressed into a tight line, but his eyes—they smiled. He thought he'd won. "This was your idea," he said, his voice equally quiet. "Put everyone in the spotlight so we could tease out the real murderer using logic and evidence. I wonder what you think of your idea now."

"Thank you for your input," Benji said loudly. "But we haven't gotten to everyone yet." He turned to Jasmine. "Why don't we move on to you? You dated Ranger Eric long distance, and it didn't end well. You came here to confront him. Mind telling us about that?"

Jasmine's gaze jumped from Mr. Harding back to Benji in surprise at the abrupt change of focus and the attention that was now on her. Moisture sprang to her eyes, and she gave an almost imperceptible nod. "I do mind."

"Is there any reason we shouldn't suspect you in either of these deaths?" Benji asked.

Jasmine opened her mouth, but no sound came out. After a long moment of uncomfortable silence, she finally said, "I hated...Eric. He made a fool of me. He played me, and I wanted him to look at me and admit what he'd done. Hard to do that if he's dead."

"Maybe you just couldn't wait anymore," Amber said, seeming anxious to cling to anyone other than herself who might have a motive.

"I still loved him," she insisted. "In a way. And I certainly wouldn't do anything that would trap us down here."

I raised my hand as if we were back in school. "That's been bothering me. Why kill our guide? There is no sense to it. Even if Jasmine had wished him harm, she wouldn't sacrifice her self-interest. Even if she felt an all-consuming passion overcome her and she had to lash out, she would have already had to have had a plan in place. That's not a crime of passion.

"First, there's the flashlight. She couldn't have stolen it in the dark. When our headlamps are turned off, our eyes don't adjust. She needed to already have the flashlight and know exactly where he was positioned so she could do everything in one fluid motion."

"You don't think Jasmine is capable of all that," Mr. Harding said, looking amused. Almost like he knew something I didn't.

"Not unless she's an incredible actress," I said. "Yesterday, my family saw firsthand how she reacts to even the possibility of being in the dark. It renders her immobile. If she were going to kill him, she wouldn't have chosen a thousand feet underground."

Amber held up a finger. "So, you're saying her sister would have done it for her."

I hadn't been, but it did get the wheels turning. "You do always take care of Jasmine, don't you?" I said, turning to Violet. "You came along on this trip because your sister begged you to be a support for her. You're the one who helps her up when she falls down and gives her the courage to do what needs to be done. Jasmine wanted to back out of it, but you said you'd come too far. She had to finish what she'd started."

"Yes, by confronting the man," Violet said. "Not by murdering him. And honestly, I don't think she's capable of either."

"Charlie, what do you think?" I said, turning to him. "You're a guide here at the caverns. How difficult would it be to murder someone in the dark with your flashlight?"

Ranger Charlie looked like he'd been caught in headlights, like he'd been hoping to stay under the radar and out of this conversation entirely. "I wouldn't know," he said, his voice shaking. "This is the first tour I've ever done, and they didn't cover murder tactics in orientation."

"But do you think it is possible that Jasmine or Violet could have murdered Eric?" Amber asked with a hint of hope in her voice.

Charlie shook his head slowly. "Now, I'm not one to throw around accusations. I'm not an expert at these things, and I didn't see anything happen." He paused and sucked in a long breath, maybe hoping we'd forget about him in the brief interlude. "However, if I were going to take a wild and completely unfounded guess, I might be inclined to think it was Mr. Harding. He notices everything and likes to pit people against each other, effectively keeping himself out of things." He threw a nervous look at the journalist, maybe worried he would be struck down for voicing his opinion. "But what do I know? It's my first day here."

19

We all stared at the ranger, who sat there, trembling.

"Those were some interesting observations," Violet finally said, turning to the journalist. "Care to give us your thoughts?"

Mr. Harding seemed nonplussed as usual and smoothed down his jacket, his signature smile in place. "Of course I notice things. That's what I do. I wouldn't have a job otherwise. As far as pitting you all against each other, you do that just fine without me. It's been Maddie, your resident psychologist, who has been pulling people out for one-on-ones, getting you to spill your darkest secrets. And then she uses that against you."

I stayed silent, knowing that anything I said could only make things worse. When I didn't take the bait, Mr. Harding felt the need to fill the silence by further defending himself. It worked every time with my patients, and as much as he liked to think otherwise, he was no different.

"Besides," he said, "what reason could I possibly have for killing two people and trapping us down here?"

"That's the thing," I said, my annoyance rising. I tried to keep a cool composure like Mr. Harding. It was his confidence that made people want to believe him, and getting antsy wouldn't work in my favor. But looking at his smug grin, I was losing the battle. I squeezed my eyes shut, forced a deep breath, and then tried again.

"No one has motive to trap us down here. That would be crazy. And no one person has motive to kill both of the men. So, forgive me, Mr. Harding, but your lack of motivation means nothing right now. Because even without it, two men are dead."

"Then I suggest you apply Occam's razor," the journalist said, motioning toward the others in the group.

Lilly nodded in understanding. "The simplest explanation is usually the correct one. And in this case, that would mean we have two murderers. Jasmine killed Eric, and Amber killed Thomas."

"But I didn't," they both yelled simultaneously, jumping forward, their eyes wild.

I held up a hand to calm them. "I understand Occam's razor, and I do think it is useful in many situations," I told Mr. Harding. "But life is far from simple. We can't condemn these two women because it's the easy way out or because we don't want to take the time to dig deeper."

"Which proves what I've been saying all along," Charlie said, speaking up. "That Dr. Swallows didn't do it. If she had, she'd have let Jasmine and Amber take the fall. But she wants to dig deeper, and Mr. Harding doesn't want her to. Which proves that he did it." He looked at me with a big smile, as if wanting me to tell him he'd done a good job.

I appreciated Charlie trying to help. He was a sweet kid who had something to prove and was trying to figure out how to come into his own. But unfortunately, his logic was just as faulty as Mr. Harding's.

"Thank you for your vote of confidence," I said to Charlie. I turned to the others. "But no, it doesn't prove anything, though I will admit that Mr. Harding's behavior does seem suspicious."

I looked at each of the people gathered around me. "This isn't going to work. We can look at each other and point fingers all day, but in the end, it doesn't prove anything."

"Too bad we don't have any evidence," Mr. Harding said. "That would make things so much simpler. Oh wait, we do. When I suggested the use of Occam's razor, I didn't mean the ex-girlfriends were guilty."

He had been referring to Flash. The one who'd had the evidence literally in his pocket.

"Like I said, life is more complex than that," I said, my

voice low. Some might have interpreted it as threatening. I hoped Mr. Harding did.

I was saved from his rebuttal when voices interrupted us from our left. People were coming. But they couldn't have found us this quickly. By my calculations, the tour would have only finished twenty minutes earlier.

"I found them," a woman called. Lights bobbed into view, but I couldn't tell who was attached to them. "What are you guys doing here? You should have already finished, and you're barely into the tour."

We all looked at each other, and then to the two men lying on the cavern floor.

The woman's gaze followed ours, and then her hand flew to her mouth. "No." She dropped to the floor. "No, no, no. It's not possible." It was only then that I recognized her as the receptionist who had help me purchase our tickets.

Two men joined the receptionist a moment later. They wore ranger jackets, and their gazes immediately sought out Charlie.

"What happened?" a tall one asked gruffly.

Charlie opened his mouth but once again was struck silent, all confidence gone. His gaze dropped to the cavern floor, as if this had been his fault.

Mr. Harding took it upon himself to step forward and speak for the group. Of course he did. And I was terrified of what he might have to say.

"We don't know," I interrupted, hurrying toward the rangers. One of the men was the ranger who had helped direct my family to the elevator the previous day. "When we all turned our lights off for part of the demonstration, Ranger Eric was hit from behind. The tape from the cavern floor has been removed, and we didn't want to get lost trying to find our way out, so we decided to stay here until someone noticed we were missing. Thomas died from an injection about an hour later. We haven't been able to figure out who is responsible."

The words tasted bitter on my tongue.

I looked to Mr. Harding, curious if he was going to contradict me. His gaze met mine. And then he looked away. "I'll be printing a story on my experience here," he told the rangers. "Considering this is a firsthand account, it would be irresponsible not to. I would appreciate your cooperation in any further questions I might have."

He wasn't going to push an arrest. Wasn't going to throw Flash under the bus. Why?

Or would that come later? In his story.

The receptionist threw Mr. Harding a glare that would have caused me to wither on the spot. Of course, he wasn't the least bit fazed by it.

"Your 'story,'" she did air quotes, "is the least of my concerns right now. And you can count on me giving your name to the police as a person of interest."

It looked like the receptionist didn't have any patience for journalists, and for the first time since arriving, Mr. Harding didn't know what to say.

The receptionist smirked, then glanced back at the two

rangers. "I'm going to lead these folks out of here and radio for the police. I think we best leave Eric and our expired guest alone until then. Please stay down here to make sure nothing is disturbed. The police will take over when they arrive. If they need any further help, they'll ask."

The rangers nodded in agreement.

The receptionist spun toward us. "I'm Sarah, and I'll be taking care of you today. I can't imagine the morning you've had, but we'll need to take a statement from everyone before you are allowed to leave. Lunch will of course be provided as we sort all this out." She looked to Charlie. "I'll need you to bring up the rear and make sure we all stay together. No one strays."

Even though one of us was a murderer, she wanted to keep us happy, because I'd imagine two dead bodies was a public relations nightmare.

Flash looked thrilled at the thought of free food, and I had no doubt he'd be quite content for as long as it took. He was probably hoping it would take long enough that dinner would be offered as well.

Charlie looked less thrilled at the prospect of being at the back of the pack, but he nodded and took his place.

"Are you a ranger?" I asked Sarah, quickening my steps so we could walk in sync. "You found us so quickly. We didn't think you'd notice our absence for at least another hour."

Sarah glanced at me. "I'm not a ranger, though I'd like to be. I'm the assistant park manager, though it seems I do a little bit of everything nowadays, and I was the one who took the call. I don't normally handle these sorts of things, but Eric... He was a friend. I wasn't going to be left behind if something was wrong."

I had so many questions about that simple statement. Better start with the obvious. "Someone called and told you we were missing?" I asked. There was no way anyone down there had cell reception.

Sarah glanced behind her, as if to make sure Charlie was doing his job and that we were all together. Her gaze then found me. "You're Maddie Swallows, right?"

"Yes," I said slowly, fairly certain she hadn't memorized the guest log. She hadn't even asked what Thomas's name was, and he was dead. She'd simply referred to him as "the guest."

Sarah managed a smile. "Your mother called and said she was worried. The tour should have ended eleven minutes earlier, and you weren't answering your phone." Her smile faded. "Normally I wouldn't have thought anything of it. Many of our rangers go over time with their tours. But never Eric. If we were lucky, he ended on time, but more often than not, he ended his tours early. When he didn't answer on his radio, I gathered a couple of rangers to come look for you."

I had never loved my mother more than in that moment. God bless her and her suffocating ways. Her constant worry had driven me nuts as a teenager, and many times as an adult, if I was being honest. I hadn't realized until the past few years that her relentless worrying and need for control actually masked an intense love, and it was her love that had saved us today.

"I'll never complain about my mom interfering ever again," I said with a small laugh. In actuality, I probably would. That was what kids did, right? Even the forty-three-year-old ones. Especially considering how many opinions she'd had in regard to my upcoming wedding, and how many she'd likely still try to sneak in.

We approached one of the ladders, and Sarah climbed up first.

"You sure know your way around this place, even without the tape on the ground," I said. "You sure you're not a ranger?"

Sarah hesitated at the top and motioned for me to climb next. "Eric and I... We were close. He knew I was frustrated that I kept getting passed over for the ranger position, even though I meet all the requirements. I prefer to be in the thick of things, rather than stuck behind a desk. So, he'd bring me on the tours sometimes. Train me. When the time is right, I'll be ready and will hit the ground running."

My confusion must have been obvious, because Sarah laughed as Lilly climbed the ladder behind me. "I know he seems like the last person you'd want for a friend, but if you managed to get on his good side, he'd never let you down. He was the best guy here." She paused, and moisture filled her eyes. "I never thought I'd have to refer to him in the past."

"So...you weren't his girlfriend?"

Sarah gave me a funny look. "He wasn't dating anyone, as far as I know."

20

"You're sure Eric wasn't dating anyone?" I asked Sarah. It was plausible that he just hadn't shared details about his love life with his co-worker. He and Sarah may have been friends, but Eric didn't seem like the kind of guy who openly shared every aspect of his life.

"No time for dating. He was always here, even on his days off. Wasn't supposed to be here today, but apparently took one of the other rangers' shifts without me knowing." Sarah's eyes filled with moisture again, and her voice dropped to a whisper. "Why was the idiot here today of all days?"

I gave her a kind smile. "On our tour, I could hear the passion in his voice when he talked about the history of the caverns, and the formations. This where he belonged." I paused. "Maybe he was better suited for online dating. Something that would fit with his work schedule a bit better."

That made Sarah laugh, and her expression opened. It was nice to see. "Eric may look young, but in his heart, he's closer in age to Ralph, our seventy-five-year-old volunteer. Eric always liked to do things old-school. He still has a landline in his apartment, believe it or not. And an answering machine. He was okay with the radios we use for work, but he didn't like how accessible cell phones make people. Social interaction wasn't exactly his strong suit, and he liked to be able to check out when he needed to."

I quirked my eyebrows. "He must have had a computer, though. And internet."

"Well, sure," Sarah said, looking past me to the ladder. Charlie was just bringing up the rear now, and she spun around to move on to the next ladder. "He had all that, but he'd never use it for online dating. He used it for email, mostly. Eric didn't have any social media accounts, and he still read a newspaper for his news—like an actual newspaper. I didn't know they still printed those until I saw him reading it at work one day."

This made no sense. Why would someone want him dead?

Unless they hadn't.

It had been a mistake.

"Eric was standing next to Thomas," I murmured.

Sarah glanced back. "Sorry?"

"No one wants to leave behind evidence, even if planting it on someone else. There's always a risk it will lead back to you. The syringe was plan B."

She stopped completely and turned to me. "Do you know who killed Eric?"

I thought I might know, but I immediately second-guessed myself. There were so many loose ends.

"Yesterday, Eric said there were no openings on the tour. He didn't want us down here." I looked at Sarah. "Why would he do that unless he knew something was going to happen?"

I expected Sarah to look equally perplexed. Instead, panic burst across her features. Fear. She refused to look at me as we walked, her steps quickening. She didn't so much as glance back to see how the rest of the group was getting on.

"He's as good a man as they make them—too good sometimes," she said, her words quick, her expression conflicted.

What Sarah was trying to tell me lay in what she wasn't saying. She wanted me to know the truth, even if she couldn't find the courage to say it outright.

"What do you know, Sarah?" I asked. "Eric knew something bad was going to happen. How?"

Sarah stopped midstep, squeezing her eyes shut and pulling in a long breath. When she resumed walking, her voice had dropped so low, I had to strain to hear her. "I saw someone emerging from the lower cave entrance early yesterday morning, before we opened. They had no reason to be there. I told Eric what I saw, worried I'd forgotten to lock a gate the previous evening. It's my responsibility to double-check that we're all locked up after closing. Eric had taken Charlie down the night before to help acquaint him with the Lower Cave tour, but I swear it was locked after they finished. He said not to worry, but his eyes said otherwise. He was concerned."

"And you didn't stop and question this person when you saw them?" I asked. "They were probably the one who removed the tape."

Sarah squeezed her hands into fists, battling the emotions that were threatening to explode. "I know I should have. But it was dark and I was alone. The way they were sneaking around—" Her voice hitched. "I'm not equipped to deal with those kinds of people. I called for security, but by the time they arrived, the person had disappeared. Couldn't find them anywhere."

I raised an eyebrow but stayed quiet. There was no sense in laying any more blame—it wouldn't help anything. Whatever Sarah had done or hadn't done, we had to focus on what would happen over the next twenty minutes.

"One of the people with us right now is a murderer," she continued. "Two people are dead, and it's my fault."

"Sarah, you can't blame yourself—"

She threw her arms into the air. "Yes, I can." She'd accidentally shouted that last part, and it echoed off the rock around us.

"Everything okay up there?" Mr. Harding called from somewhere in the rear. I glanced back and saw Lilly and Flash trailing behind, with Benji a couple of people behind them. It seemed they knew something was happening up here and were purposely holding the group up. And I loved them for it.

"Everything's fine," I called back. "We're getting close to being out of here."

"Thank goodness," Violet said from behind Flash. "I'm so cold, I can hardly feel my toes."

I turned back to Sarah. "Did Eric come down here after you told him what you saw?"

Sarah nodded. "We're not supposed to be down here by ourselves, though, so he didn't go far enough to notice the missing tape. Just far enough to make sure the rope and ladders were intact. Safety precautions, you know. He suspected graffiti and possibly drug paraphernalia would be discovered on your tour today, maybe even theft of stalactites or other delicate formations, and wanted to limit the number of people coming down here until they knew what they were dealing with. Our manager refused to allow the tour to be canceled based on conjecture, though. People travel from all over the world to be here, and we only close something down if there is a real risk."

I thought back to our tour. Eric hadn't seemed the least

surprised by the missing tape. "He knew," I said. "Maybe he didn't know the specifics, but he knew they'd find something amiss when we went down into the Lower Cave today. That was why he came in on his day off and led the tour himself."

Sarah squared her shoulders, refusing to look at me as she led me to the second ladder. "He's that kind of person —or he was. And now he's dead because of me. I shouldn't have said anything."

"Then a different ranger would have been down here, and if they were the one to die, you'd be blaming yourself for staying silent," I said. "It was a lose-lose situation."

She glanced back at me, biting her lip. "You're saying that no matter what anyone did, someone was going to die today?" She looked like she might have a panic attack, and this moment couldn't be a worse time for it. "I might have sold a tour ticket to the killer. Or maybe I noticed some-thing that I've forgotten or—"

"Sarah," I said, my voice soft. "I think I already know who killed him. But I need you to hold it together for a little longer. Before we do anything, we're going to need backup."

21

The moment Sarah heard that I thought I knew who the killer was, she asked, "Then what are we still doing here?" Her steps quickened. "I already radioed for someone to call the police. They should be meeting us at the exit."

Violet overheard Sarah from where she was walking farther back in the corridor and called, "Did someone say the police will be waiting for us?"

If she'd heard that, I wondered how much else she'd overheard. Or what others who were walking closer had heard.

"The killer will panic if they think they're trapped," I said, my voice low. Then I called back, "We were saying we wish we could contact the police so they'd be waiting for us."

Flash piped up. "What would be even better would be

police officers waiting with a few extra-large pizzas at the top. I'm starving."

As if he hadn't thrown up an entire leftover pizza the day before.

I didn't know if Flash was serious or just trying to lighten the conversation to keep people from worrying, but I appreciated it, regardless.

"I think we all deserve a pizza party after what we've gone through," I said. "My treat."

My kids cheered, but they were the only ones.

In fact, even though we were on our way out of the cavern and everyone should be showing signs of relief, no one did. If anything, they looked more worried now than ever.

I was missing something. A final puzzle piece that would help everything fit together. But I only had about ten minutes to do it. Once we were out of the cavern, we'd be questioned, but then we'd be home free. The police weren't going to arrest anyone without concrete evidence. And the only thing I had was conjecture.

I glanced back. Mr. Harding's lips were pressed together in a firm line as he climbed. He seemed annoyed but not panicked. Amber had a similar look about her, though maybe a tad more nervous as she constantly looked behind her. It was as if she was making certain everyone was still there and we hadn't lost anyone else.

Then there was Jasmine and Violet.

I paused as I waited at the bottom of the last ladder.

Sarah climbed it ahead of me, but I didn't notice when she'd reached the top because I couldn't tear my gaze from the sisters. Violet looked so nervous, I wouldn't have been surprised if she puked.

And yet, Jasmine... I'd never seen her calmer.

Maybe it was because we were finally on our way out of the cavern. We had been rescued.

But I didn't think so. I'd seen many people who suffered from anxiety, and this was not a normal reaction.

"Jasmine," I said, allowing Lilly to go ahead of me so I could get closer to the redheaded sisters.

As soon as I said Jasmine's name, the anxiety returned, and she crinkled her forehead in worry as she looked my way. "What is it? Did something happen? I knew this was too good to be true. We're not getting out of here, are we?"

I cocked my head to the side. "I was just checking on you. Making sure everything's all right."

Her body relaxed, and the tension faded. "Oh, yes. I'm fine. Ranger Charlie's taking good care of us back here."

He grinned and gave me a thumbs up.

Memories of my mom helping us get ready for our trip washed over me, followed by our arrival, our orientation, and finally our harrowing ordeal in the caverns.

There would be a lot of guesswork, but I was certain I was right.

"Charlie," I said, my voice even. "Please don't allow the sisters to fall behind. Not when we're so close."

I thought I'd said it in the most nonchalant way I

could, but there must have been something in my tone—it was something even a seasoned therapist wouldn't have picked up on. But someone did.

"Charlie," Mr. Harding said. "Not only should we make sure they stay with the group, we should put them right up front. It can only help with Jasmine's fears, right?"

"Of course," Charlie said, immediately jumping into action and ushering the two sisters up. "I don't know why I didn't think of it earlier."

Mr. Harding was watching me very carefully now. Studying me. It was a challenge. He wanted to see what I was going to do next.

When Jasmine moved to pass me, I positioned my body in front of the final ladder, blocking her way. It was a risky move, but after this ladder, she'd be home free. No need for us anymore, and even though Sarah had radioed for police, I couldn't count on them already being in position.

"Jasmine, what was Eric's girlfriend's name? I don't think it came up in our session, and I've been dying to know."

She hesitated. "I don't know. In the text he called her Honey."

Sarah leaned over the top of the ladder. "What are you talking about? He wasn't dating anyone, and he certainly wouldn't text her if he was."

Jasmine looked up, annoyance crossing her features. "How would you know? You're just the receptionist."

Pink tinged Sarah's cheeks, and she spluttered, unable to find the words to defend herself.

"Assistant manager and future ranger," I corrected. "And she was in love with Eric. If I'm not mistaken, he returned her feelings."

Sarah looked perplexed as to how I could possibly know this, but then nodded. "No one else understood him. But he was kind, and generous, and even funny, though in an unintentional kind of way." Her brows furrowed. "And one of you took him from me."

"We already know it was the boy who did it," Violet said, the words bursting from her, like she couldn't say them fast enough. "We found the syringe in his pocket."

Jasmine threw her sister a look of warning, as if to say she had this covered, but Violet either didn't get the message or she was ignoring it.

"Mr. Harding was telling us all about the Swallows family," Violet continued. "They're dangerous, you know. Can't trust them. They'll stick together, have each other's backs, and then you blink, and you're dead."

Rather than being annoyed at the accusation, I actually found it quite funny. And pretty on point. I grinned. That was the opening I'd needed.

"Thank you for that little introduction," I told her. "I didn't know if you were involved, but that answered my question." I paused, gathering my thoughts. "Violet and Jasmine. Both beautiful names. I've heard another floral name recently that I quite liked. Aster. It's a lovely purple flower."

Violet's face paled.

"I'd like to introduce you to two members of the Flora crime family," I said to Sarah, who had settled in on the top rung of the ladder, with Lilly just behind her. I then turned back to the redheaded sisters. "My mom just had to tell me all about what happened to Aster as I was getting ready for this trip—arrested for something he didn't do and will likely do fifteen years in prison, isn't that right? She found the whole story fascinating."

The sisters stayed silent.

"Is he your brother?" I tried again. "Personally, I think he stole the jewelry and is trying to frame that poor employee. I hope you're a bit better at this than him, but something tells me you're not."

"Aster is our father," Violet said, which earned a glare from Jasmine. "But that doesn't tell us how you knew. A lot of people name their kids after flowers."

I nodded. "Yes, I didn't make the connection right away. But I've been watching everyone here, and you're not as afraid of the dark as you like to let on."

I glanced back at Sarah. "If it's any consolation, Jasmine didn't mean to kill Eric. She seems fairly new at this, and it's likely her first job. The moral of the story is that you should never plan to murder someone when you can't even see them."

"No, it's not any consolation," Sarah said, her eyes

narrowed as she descended the ladder, with Lilly clambering close behind, and I was worried what Sarah might do when she reached the bottom. "If she hadn't meant to kill Eric and trap herself, then why remove the tape in the first place?"

"Chaos." I glanced at Jasmine. "It's your family's jewelry store where Thomas has been working as a gemologist. And you blame him for your father's arrest. How am I doing so far?"

There was no remnant of the scared woman she'd been. Instead, something dark and fearless lurked behind her gaze. "How could you have possibly figured out any of that just because of a random news story that your aging mother happened to mention?"

"I know how people work," I said slowly, trying to choose my words wisely. I turned my gaze on Violet. "And both of your reactions have been inconsistent since you arrived here. At first, Jasmine is the one freaking out, and Violet, you're the one comforting her. I know Jasmine has been putting on a show this whole time, but I'm not so sure you were. If I'm not mistaken, Violet, you had no idea why you two were here. That's why you've been so angry since Eric's murder. Because you realized what you'd put yourself in the middle of, and Jasmine not only didn't tell you, but she dragged you along for the ride. She's the reason you're in this mess."

Violet's eyebrows scrunched together, and she glared at her sister. "She knew I wanted no part of the family business. It only brings trouble." She glanced back at me. "I'm supposed to be opening my own business, you know. A legit one. None of this jewelry stuff. But now..."

"Now that we're leaving, Jasmine is the calm one, and you're the one freaking out. Maybe because you realize Jasmine messed up. She's gotten in over her head and on her first job killed the wrong guy. She only said it was Eric she had been in an online relationship with because she didn't want to be tied to Thomas. And the Flora family doesn't respond well to mess-ups. It's not the police you're worried about. It's whoever is waiting for you." I pointed up. "Because it's not the police who will be hauling you away, is it? Not with Aster so recently being arrested. The family can't afford another incident like his splashed across the media."

Sarah's complexion paled at the thought of a mafia family waiting for us to exit the caverns and she shrunk back against the ladder, nervously looking up, as if they were already there.

"Thomas had one job to do," Jasmine spat out. "Sign the certificates. So what, we steal some of the customers' jewelry when they're brought in for repair—replace genuine items with glass. Those rich people don't know any different. Neither do their friends. It's not hurting anyone. And yet Thomas fancies himself a hero, and despite the warnings of his new *girlfriend*, he goes to the feds. And now our dad is in jail. For what?"

The way Jasmine emphasized *girlfriend*, it gave me pause.

"You really were in an online relationship with Thomas, weren't you? Probably knew of him because of the store but couldn't risk meeting in person. I'm assuming it would have been frowned upon, given his close proximity to your family. He then starts dating Amber, and suddenly you become someone he only casually talks to. This 'job' of yours is not only personal because he put your dad in prison, but because you actually cared about Thomas. Of course, when things didn't go your way, you were willing to kill him for his betrayal." I released a low whistle and shook my head. "Remind me to never get on your bad side."

"Why you—" Jasmine looked like she was going to come for me, but Benji pushed his way from the back of the group, placing himself between me and the sisters.

"You could have warned me we were doing this here," he murmured. "Violet was right about one thing—our family stands together." As if it had been planned, Flash and Lilly followed suit, planting themselves in front of me, next to Benji.

"You aren't going to kill our mom like you did Thomas," Flash said with a resolute nod.

Jasmine glared but didn't move closer. "I did not murder Thomas."

"But you were supposed to," Amber said, moving toward Jasmine, who immediately stepped back. "Why are you even down here? My father would never trust you with something like this. You're his errand girl. What you do doesn't matter."

My gaze jumped from Jasmine to Amber, my brain trying to wrap around what was happening here.

Mr. Harding yawned, like he was bored. "But she does fly under the radar."

Amber scoffed. "You mean, how she's wailing all the time and acting like the world is ending? Is that your definition of under the radar?"

I had thought I had it all worked out. But now I was just confused. "Wait, you all know each other?"

They couldn't possibly all be a part of the same family. Amber wasn't a...

I couldn't believe I hadn't seen it. "Flower carpet amber rose. My aunt had some growing in her garden."

Benji raised an eyebrow. "Seriously?"

"They are these small orange roses..." I trailed off when I realized everyone was watching me.

"We're the only ones who don't belong," Lilly said, finally understanding the magnitude of what we'd inadvertently gotten ourselves involved with. She turned to Ranger Charlie. "Even you?"

C harlie gave a vigorous shake of his head. "I don't understand anything right now." Gone was his smile, and in its place was concerned confusion.

"No one belongs here," Amber said, anger lacing her words. She spun toward Mr. Harding. "Thomas was a good guy. Yes, he was gullible. But he was smart and funny, and he didn't deserve what you did to him."

Mr. Harding gave a sad shake of his head, not like he regretted what they had done but because Amber didn't understand why they'd had to do it. "We told you not to get involved with him. It could only lead to trouble."

"Well, you shouldn't have hired him in the first place," she retorted. "We keep things in the family."

He released an exasperated sigh. "You know the community was starting to push. We needed someone to take the fall. Instead, Aster is in prison, Thomas is dead, and the feds are closing in. All because you wanted to play house with an outsider."

"You're blaming me for everything our family has done?" Amber screeched. "Like Violet, all I wanted was a normal life. And you couldn't let me have that." She caught Mr. Harding—or whatever his name really was—off guard and lunged at him, knocking him over. His head bounced off a rock, and he stilled. Her gaze was wild as she spun in a circle, looking for a way out.

It landed on me.

"I was supposed to protect him," she said. "He trusted me. And I let him down."

And then she shoved me aside, bolted past Sarah and up the ladder, and disappeared into the dark.

Violet was already by Mr. Harding's side, checking for a pulse.

Lilly crept forward. "Is he…"

Mr. Harding groaned and rolled over, sending Lilly jumping back toward us, using Benji as cover. I didn't blame her, now that we knew who he really was.

"When I get my hands on her," he grumbled.

Jasmine laughed, though it was devoid of humor. "You won't do a thing. She's the boss's daughter. He'll do what he wants, but for us, it's hands off."

Mr. Harding growled and stumbled to his feet. "He won't have a hands-off policy when it comes to you, now will he? Your first job, and you messed things up worse than Aster. The boss is going to let you take the fall for this. He'll probably call the feds himself and tell them what you've done. If you'd left the ranger alone and just done what you were supposed to—"

Jasmine paled. "It wasn't my fault. Uncle Terry—I mean, the boss—always stresses the importance of no witnesses. The ranger was suspicious from the start. I heard him talking to Charlie—he knew something wasn't right down here. It didn't matter which one of us he suspected, we'd all be in trouble if he figured out the truth."

"Okay, fine," Mr. Harding conceded. "So, you take the ranger out. But he wasn't your mark."

"I was getting to it," Jasmine insisted. "But Uncle Terry never should have sent you. I didn't need you here babysitting me, and it made me nervous."

"Good thing I was," Mr. Harding said. "Even though I'd hacked into the computer system so it thought all the tours were full for today, somehow, we still managed to have unexpected guests. How were you going to handle that?" He nodded to my family.

Jasmine barely glanced at us. "I had the psychologist fooled, and I would have gotten the job done."

"And yet you didn't," Mr. Harding said, then a little louder, "I'm a journalist so I can keep an eye on what stories people are digging up about the family. I already knew a great deal about our uninvited guests and was able to keep them at bay while I cleaned up after you. The boss didn't think you were ready for this kind of assignment, and he was right."

It took me a minute to realize it wasn't for my benefit. His pocket was lit up. He was recording. Not for a story. But so his boss would know exactly what had happened—he wanted evidence that he'd done well and didn't deserve the family wrath.

What a terrifying way to live, always having to watch your back, afraid someone will turn on you.

Speaking of someone turning on us, if we stayed any longer, the Flora family would remember they had witnesses, and as Uncle Terry always says, *No witnesses*.

I tapped the kids' shoulders and ushered them toward the ladder. Sarah still stood next to it, seemingly frozen in shock. I gestured for her to go first. She hesitated, sending a nervous glance toward the rest of the group. She must have decided she'd be more help if she were outside the cavern, because the next moment she was clambering up the rungs. Lilly and Flash had no qualms going next as they followed close on her heels.

"Go," I whispered to Benji, who looked like he was holding back, waiting for me to go first. I gave him a little push toward the ladder and threw an anxious glance over my shoulder. Now wasn't the time for my fiancé to be a gentleman.

I was halfway up when the sisters and Mr. Harding stopped arguing long enough to notice what we were doing.

"I don't think so," Mr. Harding said. With one long stride, he was by my side and lifting me off the ladder, my feet dangling midair.

I didn't know where Ranger Charlie had come from, but one minute I was praying the kids weren't watching—didn't need them to relive this moment for the rest of their trauma-filled lives—and the next, I was crashing down on top of Mr. Harding. I scurried off him and practically leaped up the ladder before squeezing myself through the narrow rocks at the top, where Benji was waiting for me. His expression held all the fear I'd felt, and he wrapped his arms around me, like I'd disappear if he let go. When I looked back, Charlie was doing some kind of kung fu moves on the sisters.

He glanced up with his characteristic grin, but then it dipped. "Eric told me just before orientation that he was expecting trouble, and he requested I be the other ranger on this tour, just in case. This is my responsibility. Go on ahead, and I'll take care of these guys." He hesitated. "But if you could tell the cops to be quick, that would be great. I'm still counting on that pizza party you promised us."

I laughed, more out of relief than anything. "I'll buy you all the pizza you want."

"Me too, right?" I heard Flash call from somewhere up ahead.

I smiled as I rolled my eyes. "Yes, you too."

Benji kissed me quickly before I grabbed the rope to pull myself out of the cavern.

"You still stressed about the wedding?" he asked with a wink to let me know he was teasing me, but it seemed to be more of a tactic to calm his own nerves.

"I don't know that I'll ever be stressed about anything again," I said, and I really meant it. After what we'd gone through that day, I was only left with gratitude. And some sadness. I hoped Amber was going to be okay. "I think we need to add a few people to our guest list, though."

I reached the top and turned to watch Benji climb up the final large rock.

"If you invite Mr. Harding, you'll need to invite the entire Flora family," he said. "They don't seem to be the type who leaves anyone out."

That wasn't exactly who I had in mind.

But speaking of the Flora family, I sincerely hoped that if members of the crime organization were waiting for us when we exited, it would be someone more like Amber and less like Mr. Harding.

BENJI and I stood at the gate we'd entered several hours earlier. It felt like days. Police officers surrounded us, preparing to descend into the cavern, but in all the chaos, I couldn't find Flash or Lilly. It took a few minutes to realize they weren't even there.

Panic rose in my chest. But then I heard the single most beautiful word that existed.

"Grandma!"

Flash and Lilly rounded a bend in the path that led to the elevators, my mom walking between them.

"Oh, thank goodness you're all right," my mom said, limping toward me and wrapping me in her arms. Her knees were not made for places like Carlsbad Caverns. "I don't know what happened down there, but according to your children, it seems to have something to do with a mob boss and some flowers. Poisonous, I can only assume."

"Something like that," I said, hugging her tight. "How did you get here so quickly? That's a three-hour drive."

My mom tapped her forehead. "A mother always knows when her daughter is in trouble."

I didn't buy it for a minute.

She gave me a guilty smile. "That, and I got lonely and thought I would surprise you. I know this was supposed to be a family trip with just your kids and Benji, but it didn't feel right, being left behind. And I was mad at you."

The way she said it, I didn't think it was supposed to be funny, but I couldn't help but laugh. It always drove me nuts how she interjected herself into every aspect of my life. I complained constantly about how she couldn't give me space for even a day. And yet, I wouldn't have it any other way.

"I am glad you're here, Mom, but just because you managed to rescue us this one time, it doesn't give you permission to hijack every family vacation we take."

My mom only smiled.

And then more police showed up, sprinting from the opposite direction, with Sarah following close behind. "Where's Charlie?" she asked, her breaths coming fast.

"Still down there. You need to hurry, because I don't know how long he can hold Mr. Harding and the sisters off." I paused. "He saved my life."

"You heard her," Sarah yelled over the commotion. "Forget protocol. You need to get down there, and now."

The officers blinked a couple of times, having no idea who either of us was but must have determined that it didn't matter, because whoever must have been in charge gave the order, and they pressed ahead and down the rock face.

Flash clapped his hands together. "Now, about that lunch we were promised."

L illy's knees bounced up and down, her camera in one hand. "When's it going to start?"

"The pamphlet says approximately twenty-two minutes past sunset," I said, reading one of the many free brochures I'd picked up from the gift shop over the past few days. "It's not like you can demand they start on your schedule, though."

We sat on stone benches in an amphitheater that faced the natural cave's entrance. Had we hiked down to the Big Room a couple of days earlier, this was where we would have entered. Tonight, we were here for a completely different reason.

Benji leaned forward and squinted, mirroring Lilly. "I think I see one," he said. I smiled, loving how excited he still got about simple things.

"That's just a bird," Flash said. "The cave swallows build mud nests in the mouth of the cave, remember? The movie in the visitor's center said they migrate here each year, just like the bats. It's amazing, really, how many animals can share the same habitat."

I raised an eyebrow, not having realized Flash had even been paying attention.

He lifted a shoulder and smiled. "What? I listen."

My mom snorted. "Well, that's a first."

"Mom, be nice. You invited yourself to our family vacation—you're not allowed to insult your grandkids while you're here."

She gave Flash a smile that told me she wasn't sorry but she'd pretend to be. "Your mom is right, and I shouldn't act so surprised. If you're smart enough to graduate early and get hired on by those bigwigs, you're smart enough to learn about some cave birds."

Flash grinned. "Heck yeah, I am."

A few more black shapes emerged from the cave, and Lilly excitedly lifted her camera. "Those aren't swallows."

I was tempted to think they were, but then more came out. Gradually, the number increased until thousands of bats were pouring from the mouth of the cave. The same cave we'd explored multiple times that week. A shiver moved up my spine at the thought of us occupying the same space as all those bats. Even though I knew they lived in the deepest caverns that visitors were allowed nowhere near, I couldn't help but imagine them watching us as we'd walked through the dark corridors.

And there were a lot of them.

"How many does it say live in these caves?" I wondered aloud, attempting to read my brochure in the dwindling light.

Flash looked up at the sky, as if trying to remember if the movie had given the answer to that particular question. "Between two hundred and five hundred thousand, depending on the night. I think. I'm pretty sure that's what one of the plaques said."

So, my son was capable of both reading plaques and paying attention to an educational movie. Maybe he really would be okay out in the world on his own.

Lilly was taking pictures at lightning speed, attempting to catch every moment as the bats continued to swirl out of the cave and into the night sky. Their black bodies formed a funnel, and the sky appeared to have been engulfed in a dark tornado.

The entire experience couldn't have lasted more than fifteen minutes, but it felt like an eternity. We sat in our seats long after the bats had left in search of food for the evening, too awe-struck to leave and not wanting to break the spell they had woven around us.

"What do you think?" Benji finally asked, turning to the kids. "Was this vacation enough of an adventure to cure your mom's anxiety about the wedding?"

I stared. "You can't be serious. We almost died yesterday. Two people actually did. And I just discovered we'd been sharing the caverns with hundreds of thousands of bats. The last thing I'm thinking about is our wedding. I'm just grateful that my family gets to live another day."

Benji winced and threw me a look of guilt. "You're right. Too soon to joke about what's happened. I guess I was trying to find a way to tell you that I'm so grateful for you and the kids, and this moment right here—it's perfect. I wouldn't want it any other way. Except, you know, without the near-death experience."

"You'll notice he didn't exclude me from his perfect moment," my mom said with a large smile. "Looks like I've won him over, after all."

Benji laughed. "Of course you have. You've always been like a second mom to me, and you make wonderful memories even better."

"This one's a keeper," my mom whispered to me, though purposely loud enough for everyone to hear. "Don't mess this one up."

I groaned but then reminded myself that my mom had saved our lives just yesterday. "I'm not planning on it, Mom."

She grinned. "Good. Now let's talk color coordination for your wedding. I know you're planning on blue, black, and white, but that all seems a bit dark for me. I hope you don't mind, but I've taken the liberty of ordering some yellow accents to brighten things up a bit—"

I tuned her out. Fine. We could have yellow. It didn't

matter to me anymore, because my family was going to be there when I said yes to my forever person.

And that was the only thing that mattered.

After what we'd been through, nothing could ruin my wedding day.

EPILOGUE

Was a person's wedding day ever truly their own?

I watched as yellow tablecloths replaced the white ones I'd ordered. It was fine. No big deal. My mom had overstepped her bounds, but three weeks earlier I'd determined that if the day ended with Benji as my husband, the rest didn't matter.

It turned out I did care. But just a little. This was a day for others to celebrate us as a family, and if that meant yellow tablecloths and balloons, fine.

Twenty round tables sat under a large white tent that had been erected in a field next to the town's one and only church, and a stage was being set up on the far end, complete with actual speakers. Amor was used to tiny karaoke speakers at our town events, so our wedding was already being touted as the most extravagant wedding to ever occur in our small town.

"Honey, what are you doing out here?" my mom asked, hurrying over to me. "You should be inside, getting dressed. You're getting married in the church in an hour, and you haven't touched your hair or makeup."

Oh, right. I supposed I should at least pretend to care about those things today of all days. Usually, I spent five minutes on my hair and called it a day. When I was feeling extra ambitious, I might get crazy and apply a little eyeliner and mascara.

"Don't worry, Grandma. I'll take care of her," Lilly said, approaching me. She looked gorgeous in a floor-length jade dress, her hair piled on top of her head. If she'd been wearing white, our guests could have easily mistaken her for the bride, as opposed to the woman who was still wearing sweatpants and had her hair in a ponytail.

"I did shower this morning," I said, as if that were any consolation.

My roommate, Trish, approached, looking just as stunning as my daughter, though she wore her pink-streaked hair down. It was the perfect contrast to her blue strapless dress. "It's true. She did shower," she said with a smile. "But I agree with your mom. You should probably go slightly above and beyond applying deodorant." She took one of my arms, and Lilly grabbed the other. "We'll make a bride out of you yet."

Trish agreeing with my mom. That was a first.

"And what a lovely bride she makes," a man to my right

said. I glanced his way and paused. I didn't recognize him, and yet, there was something vaguely familiar about him.

Something crashed behind me, and I whipped around to find my mother surrounded by shards of broken ceramic. She'd dropped one of the centerpieces for the tables.

"Mom?" I asked, instantly concerned. I tore my arms from Trish and Lilly's grasp and hurried over to her. "What's wrong?"

Her gaze was frozen on the man who had entered the tent. "You're not wanted here," she said, her voice hoarse. "You need to leave."

My gaze jumped from my mom to the man and back again. "Who is he?" I asked.

The man chuckled. "You mean, she's never shown you pictures of your dear old dad? It's expected, but still, a shame."

My chest constricted.

Dad?

My father had come to my wedding? He hadn't bothered to come to my first wedding. Never reached out when his grandchildren were born. I had no memories of even meeting the man. Ever.

Why now?

My mom straightened and placed herself between me and the man who claimed to have donated his DNA to my existence. "I don't know how you found out about the wedding, but you weren't invited."

The man held up his hands. "I mean no trouble."

That may have been true. He seemed sincere when he said it.

THAT WASN'T VERY comforting when Benji and I weren't even able to make it through our vows before my father jumped from the pew he'd been sitting in, screaming and hollering. He made it halfway down the aisle before he collapsed.

There was nothing the paramedics could do for him.

Murder, they said.

I shouldn't have been surprised that something like this would happen on my wedding day. But I couldn't help it.

My father was dead before I'd even learned his name.

And there was only one person I knew who hated him enough to kill him.

The End

CHOOSE YOUR OWN ADVENTURE: MYSTERY OR ROMANCE

MADDIE SWALLOWS MYSTERIES

Dead Before Dinner

Dead Upon Arrival

Dead Before I Do

Dead Among Stars

Dead by Design

Dead in the Dark

Dead Without a Hitch

BORROWING AMOR: New Mexican Romance

Borrowing Amor

Borrowing Love

Borrowing a Fiancé

Borrowing a Billionaire

Borrowing Kisses

Borrowing Second Chances

STARLIGHT RIDGE: Beach Romance

Diving into Love

Resisting Love

Starlight Love

ABOUT THE AUTHOR

Kat Bellemore is the author of both the Borrowing Amor small town romance series and the Maddie Swallows cozy mystery series. Deciding to have New Mexico as the setting for these series was an easy choice, considering its amazing sunsets, blue skies and tasty green chile. That, and she currently lives there with her husband and two cute kids. They hope to one day add a dog to the family, but for now, the native animals of the desert will have to do. Though, Kat wouldn't mind ridding the world of scorpions and centipedes. They're just mean.

You can visit Kat at www.kat-bellemore.com.